U Me & Fate

U Me & Fate

Binds & Breaks

RUCHI BHANDARI

PARTRIDGE

A Penguin Random House Company

To order additional copies of this book, contact
Partridge India
000 800 10062 62
orders.india@partridgepublishing.com

www.partridgepublishing.com/india

Contents

All's well that ends well

It is so unquestionably that our fate is not tied to anyone. If people wish to go let them go. It just means that there presence in our story is over. I was not ready to accept this fact. Every hour, every minute, all the day of my life I would feel sad for the emptiness in my life.

In the meantime I was regular to the restaurants; to open chains of restaurants in whole country was one of my top priorities. As the time started to fade, my dream also started to fade. As being unaware of the business and latest development, I was not competent to cope up with the work of pressure. In spite of continuously efforts to handle the restaurants, it did not turn out to give fruitful results.

The staffs were not receiving regular payments. Bonus was delayed for the year and after that no bonus was declared. Customers and employees were not pleased by the performance. The share price started showing a downward trend. Gradually the interest of the loan started increasingly. Payments for the interest were delaying. Repeated threatening calls were received from the banks to pay the debt. Within a meantime the restaurant started appearing empty.

10.00 A.M. just arrived at the restaurant to collect some property papers so that would be able to free the restaurant from the clutches of the banks. Searching thorough various files, there was a knock. I turned behind to see who was waiting outside and on my surprise the bank manager paid me surprise visit while carrying high voltage of rage on his face.

Could sense why the bank manager visited the restaurant early morning.

1. All he wanted to see how the working condition of the restaurant was was?
2. Would I be able to pay on time all the debts?
3. If the auction would be conducted will the bank fetch out the required amount of cash and so on?

Paused for a while I interrupted exasperatingly, "Please come in". He walked inside and sat while adjusting himself in front of my desk.

Before the muscles of my mouth could move and I could utter something he spoke in a rough tone, "Miss Tasha Growel you must be aware why I am here this morning?"

I "hmm" in response painting some sadness on my face.

Further he continued catching the highest speed, "That if the debts are not paid in time. The bank will take the restaurant in possession and go for an auction and recover the debt amount."

Frankly I wasn't surprise by the manager's visit nor did his words surprise me. All I could say after gathering all my courage was, "Samir's dad would like to meet once to all the top most bank authorities regarding the loan."

With some frown lines on his forehead and a smirk on his lips he looked at me with confusion, he said, "Alright Miss Tasha, I'll communicate to all the bank officers and try to arrange a meeting." Stood up from his sit and was about to leave.

I muttered, "Thank you." He responded the same and left.

There was a huge soulful cry that cannot be expressed by me. After the bank manager left I zipped my handbag, closed the restaurant's office and made my way through the gloomy street towards church. Fear began to race through me, yet I tried to tranquil myself from this circumstances.

Entered the church, folded my hands and prayed to Jesus. In my childhood heard fairy tales, that Jesus sends his angels to wipe the tears of his devotees and shower blessings and happiness and take away all there sufferings. I prayed "Dear God, if listening – than please bless with some brightness in these gloomy hours. Please send a small ray of hope. Please please please"

A tear rolling down while praying and did not even realize someone else were even sitting in the church. Quickly I finished my prayer and was about to leave, suddenly noticed someone there at distance was observing me, the image was blur.

I squint my eyes, what I could figure out was his physical appearance, tall and well shaped posture, strong built dressed in black and an unusual decorated blue diary in hands hold my eyes to it. The decoration on the diary wasn't girlish but was something unique and elegant captivating my eyes towards it.

Peered outside the church window, it was getting a little dark. The gray clouds covered the sun and I silently prayed to God, "Please…Please don't rain till the time I reach home."

I gather my attention, left from the church, walked towards the town market. Tensed about the present situation, weeping deep inside the heart and was threatened that tears don't come out from my eyes, quickly collected fruits and vegetables hastily toddle towards my residence. While moving towards my home abruptly I collide to someone and all my fruits and vegetables drop down from my arms and they started dancing on the street.

"Ehhh… I groaned in irritation.

Without even wasting a single minute, I infuriatingly started collected all the vegetables and fruits laying unknown on the street.

I heard a voice saying "Madam, I am extremely sorry for the trouble" and he started to help me in picking up the vegetables and fruits.

As I was weeping did not even bother myself to look up and notice the person.

Someone screamed from far-off, "Hey buddy, come fast getting late". The call was for the person who actually dashed with me and after that helping me. He replied, "Coming one moment, please".

He answered again "Madam; I'm so sorry" and rushed towards his friends. Till that moment I was just busy in gathering all the veggies and fruits.

I did not even thought to reply and give an answer to the person as was lost in the deep ocean of sorrow. After collecting all the vegetable and fruit, was about to leave for my home. Suddenly my eyes get struck towards a decorated blue diary which was resting on the street.

It was the same diary that I happen to see in the church, but could not figure out the owner of the diary. Turned behind to look for the person so that I could return him the diary but on my surprise there was no one in the street. So in that case, I decided to carry the diary along with me.

I arrived home around 8.00 pm. Mom and my younger sister Jiya were preparing the dinner.

Greeted them both, placed my keys and handbag of fruits and vegetables on kitchen counter and headed myself for a refreshing shower.

In the meantime Jiya screamed, "Come fast, the food is ready. I am dying of hunger."

"Yes, my hyperbole statement using sister," I winked while saying.

Being sister's we both look alike because we're both tall, fair and carrying a perfect slim body. But being precise we carry a lot of differences too. While Jiya had curly thick strong colored hair, mine is longer, lighter and straight. And she has deep brown eyes, and mine were the casual black but big well shaped almond eyes.

After the shower I walked towards the living room and settled myself on the couch while switching the television.

Jiya asked, "How was work?

"Busy, tiring and unexpected" I replied.

"Unexpected? Why? She frowned. I understood her confusion and made her sit beside me.

And answered, "Yeah, bank manager paid me a surprised visit"

1 - "What?"

2 - "What happened?"

3 - "What did he say?"

And so many questions went on in her mind.

I answered, "Relax, the banks have provided with a legal notice of two months to pay the debt or else they will seal the restaurants and recover the debt by selling the property."

Mom was patiently listening to our talks. Mom suddenly, interrupted and broke the bars of words between me and Jiya, and said, "don't loose hopes sweeties. Every square will settle in its proper place. All our sorrows and sufferings will come to an end".

Apparently all the past memories were often visible on my face, and she later understood and made me explain that it would be a nice if I would try and dare to face out new challenges for life.

Have faith in God was her last sentence.

"I agreed" I admitted in a soft voice, covering my face with my hands. In that mean while Jiya answered, "now only an angel can descend and shower some magic and than some miracle can save the three remaining restaurants".

After hearing this, along with tears a sweet smile broke out from my lips.

I stood up and hugged her for her innocent thought. As I always feel angels and devils appear only in movies rather than in real life.

There Jiya speaks about an angel and here on the door knock hits of the devil. Jiya rushed towards the door and I headed towards the dinning table to help mom to serve the food. After few seconds a strong arm slung over my shoulder and I looked up to meet the tall, dark and strong masculine body of my childhood best friend; KABIR.

Since school days he carried that bad boy image but with me he was at his best skills of being a gentleman. He wears stylish clothes and spends more time in mirror than I and Jiya can spend. In all he was weird, but the cutest friend of mine.

"Hey Kabira." I smirked after saying.

"Ew, you know I hate that style when you call my name weirdly."

"Yeah, that's why she calls you with that name!" Jiya responded. He gave a death glare to Jiya and stated with a teasing tone, "Shut up, you little pussy." This little conversation made me and mom laugh.

"Come, sit and join the dinner." Mom invited. Kabir occupied the chair next to me while mom and Jiya occupied the opposite chairs.

During the dinner time, often Jiya used to lift her head and glance at Kabir while pasting a sweet smile on her thin pink lips. Whether she admits or not, she had crush on Kabir. Though Kabir was my childhood best friend but it was my little sister, who knows his likes and dislikes.

"Finish your bite first, than stare." I winked while teasing her.

Jiya gave me a blank stare and responded instantly with gulping the food at once. Laugh found its way on my face. While Kabir and mom usually confused with our conversation.

"Cease your confusion" I stated while still continuing laughing.

"You sister's are terrible, any moment you can be enemies any moment best buddies" Kabir responded with irritation.

"Enjoy your dinner, or else leave Kabira, the thief." Jiya defended.

"Well, the little pussy got offended" he answered.

I let a moment pass by and let myself control my breathes of laughing.

"Chill, whatever you do, but don't mess with us." Kabir opened his mouth to protest but I cut him off. "Trust me, we sister's can be terrible to you" I answered while pointing the fork in front of him and placing it below his chin to scare him.

But before I could scare him, he instantly grabbed my wrist and said, "Touché moment, I would love to die, if the murderer is so beautiful. I love you Tasha, please don't kill me."

"Yeah…Yeah…Fine. I'll show mercy on you only if you eat the food quietly." Kabir took a pause and let out a sigh of defeat before taking his next bite.

While all were quiet, Jiya let out a laugh and shook her head, "Poor Kabira, can never win in any argument."

Kabir turned into a hot red ball of fire, before he could respond Mom interrupted, "Cease you both. And take a sip of chilled orange juice"

While taking a sip of orange juice I peered at them. They were definitely in the silence zone but constantly having an eye fight with each other. Both look adorable and where the best part of my life. Their constant fight would always distract me from my pain. My tough day would always end with such sweet and silly fights. My struggle seems to be minor destruction while these fights seem to be massive destruction.

Its perfect saying, ***"All's well that ends well."***

Capturing Time, Celebrating Milestones & Saving Memories

After completing our dinner, we all were ready to settle on our bed for sleep. It was dark outside the window. Everyone was fast a sleep but my sleep was stolen, was spinning all around the bed almost completing 360 degree by rotating round and round. Finally accepted my defeat and got up from the bed. Moving to and fro in the room, my eyes got instantly fix at the blue diary.

The blue diary had mesmerizing effects in my eyes. It had golden curved metal designed attached to its four edges. The cover page of the diary was stiff like granite stick to it. It seemed that the diary was especially designed by the owner to preserve some secrets in to it. Just there were some scratches on the granite that might be because it must have fallen down on earth or must have been dragged from some hard surface rest the book was worth preserving. The blue granite book must have some secrets to be revealed.

I was eager to open the diary and have a glance on it. But my conscious was biting me as it was some else or completely stranger's personal belongings.

There was a puzzlement in my mind should I unlock it or not. I don't know but there was some power that forced me to unlock the diary and read it.

The moment I opened the diary and began to read, I was awestruck by the frame of words by the stranger. The words were enclosed so brilliantly and placed at its proper position portraying the exact emotion. I shuffled random pages some pages were tear apart, some had half written rhymes, and some complete poems.

One poem which made my eyes stick on it and touched my emotion all through it. That moment while reading the poem, I was expression less. The poem was framed this way

TIME

Time knows best, time knows all.
Time will come when you will remember joy,
Time will come when you will forget woe.
As time knows best, time knows all.

Time knows best, time knows all.
Time will come when I will shine,
That time, the time will be mine.
As time knows best, time knows all.

Time knows best, time knows all.
Time will come when I will be in dark,
That time, the world might bark.
As time knows best, time knows all.

Time will come when I'll be weaker,
Time will come when I'll be stronger.
All I know is that time always alter.
Sometimes making it Salter, sometimes making it Sweeter.

After reading these lines the memories of my past were crystal-clear standing in front of me.

That time when I and Samir met for the first time at a common friend's birthday bash.

Samir my love….my life….we were two souls with one heart….

Early we were just friends, slowly we turned to be close friends and after sometime we decided to be soul mates.

We met at a common friend's birthday celebration. I remain very quiet at first, and Samir was of an over friendly nature exactly like a bad boy. Early his nature was annoying me, later I got along with him in a debate. After the debate which I won, he claimed "girls always win in any debate". This line made me fell, "Ahhh awful".

"Typical boy" I commented and then neglected and left for the dinner.

Despite of the disastrous dinner, Samir continued to pursue me. His action earlier where irritating me but still I was some where liking it too. In my heart I, to was even attracted towards him.

After the dine, we exchanged our cell phone numbers. Talking on the phone more in depth, exploring our backgrounds and gradually shedding our thoughts with each other.

Did not even realize when we became each others habit.

Six Years back, Tasha's birthday was an assignment for Samir. As the clock's hands meets each other i.e. 12.00am.

The door bell rang ting tong, Mom opened the door, while I was sitting in the couch of my living area relaxing and watching television turned my face to locate who has arrived in my premises so late in the night.

And I was astonish to see Samir standing at the door, holding a wild birthday hat, big bouquet of flowers and elegant diamond ring in his hand.

Mom and Jiya standing at one corner leaning towards the wall and gazing at Samir, along with all the gifts which he carried in hands.

He greeted, "Hi Tasha, How are you doing?" Slowly moved towards me, his black eyes were dazing me, and burning holes through me.

I replied softly, "Hi, I'm television", it was hard enough for me to keep myself compose under his stare.

"Err…" what I said. I'm confused.

"I mean I'm fine", I responded with perplexity.

"Happy birthday" he whispered and stayed quiet offering me nothing in return. His eyes bore into mine making my whole body shivers. Without any words he leaned and placed a tender kiss on my cheek.

Before I could reply anything, his kiss made my thoughts cease. I was completely in shock mode; my eyes were growing large and rolling all over and for that moment

I was holding my breathe and could not react at all. It made me feel as if an electrifying current have ran through all my veins and muscles making me completely dumb at the moment.

There was shyness on my face and an innocent smile which completed my emotion of happiness.

At that very moment, he dropped on one knee. Samir's intend unraveled in the shredded wrappings, holding the dazzling, one- carat, round shining diamond ring, set in platinum placed in front of me while pushing the ring in my ring finger, he proposed me. I was stunned and astonished.

Millions of thoughts were pouring in my mind. I wanted to stop this moment and preserve it till my existence. I wanted to hug him tightly, capture this time and cherish it.

Capturing Time, Celebrating Milestones, and Saving Memories was all what I wanted to do. But all I could say was just, "Thank you".

Every member of my family started laughing on me and I because of shyness could not even understand, "how to act in response"?

As I stood there for a second in a state of complete shock, I only regained control on my senses when Mom's voice registered in my brain. I quickly took my eyes off to her, and my mom standing near the kitchen door sending a small smirk to me. "Reply fast, he is on knees", she commented.

"Answer him, will you marry him?" mom asked with some sort of naughtiness in her eyes followed with a small smirk.

I slowly nodded my head with my eyes looking down to the earth saying softly, "Yes" along with satisfying smile plastered on my face.

As I finished, nobody really said anything and I think we all could all sense that the atmosphere floating around the room at the moment was definitely full of awkwardness.

Samir's eyes widened bit plastering a sweet smile on his face, breaking the deafening silence that surrounded us, "Umm...Thank You God that is all what I need?" he stood up from that bended knee, placing his hands on my waist grabbed me tightly and even I placed my arms around his neck allowing each other to embrace in our comforts.

Rewinding my self in my past memories and collecting all the enjoyable moments of my life tears started pouring out from my eyes. I did not even realize when Jiya in her sleep muttered, "Umm...Go to sleep, it late at night." That time I peered in the clock beside my bedside it was past half an hour after twelve.

I closed the blue diary, prayed to God covered my self with the blanket and shut my eyes still allowing a tear to drop out from the edge of my one eye travelling all through my cheek and falling on the pillow beneath my head.

_____XXX_____

SHOCKING MEMORIES

Zodiac Restaurant six years back was one of the leading restaurants in whole state, booming and providing a lot of employment in the country. The rates of the shares of our restaurants were very high and created high fluctuation in the stock market. Our restaurants were at its peak and everyone was happy with the progress of the restaurants.

But happiness does not come with a guarantee to stay with you for ever. Life changes and everyone have to accept the change and move on. But for me as if time was there only where Samir left me.

It what 24th days of December, 2008 were days where short and nights where long, freezing cold and windy. The snow covered the road as if the road was wrapped in the white blanket. The winds moving to and fro kissing my face and making me feel light and bright.

I rushed towards the phone to call Samir – was kind of missing him.

"Hello Honey" he answered the call in his sweet mesmerizing voice. "So you were missing me" he continued.

Hearing that line I felt as if he peered from the cell phone and was able to read my mind and judge my exact emotions.

"Yes kind of missing you only " I did not deny the fact.

"Well, in that case even I was thinking about you My Life, My Future Wife" he commented.

And I blush.

I answered, "Thinking what?"

He replied, "About our marriage, our kids… with a loud sound of muahhhhhhh….."

"EW, you went to further in your dreams." I replied with a flush on my face. I loved the way he kissed me on the phone.

Samir backfired, "Why you don't want kids?"

"Umm…yeah… I do want, I mean no." I replied in total confusion state.

"Someone on the phone is blushing around." He gestured in a teasing tone.

I voiced while carrying a blush on my face, "Take a break and listen to me."

"With full concentration I'm listening to you" he stated and definitely carrying a smirk on his face.

"Oh Samir please help me to select the color of my wedding dress?" I cry out loud, struggling for hours in selecting my dress I finally thought to disturb him only. Actually not disturb him, just wanted to hear his voice. As I said so I was missing him.

"So shall I go with red or pink?" I stated and waited for his answer.

"Umm, I guess red suits you more?" he claimed. "So, you mean pink doesn't go well with me?" I teased but carrying attitude in my words. "No no, I did not say that way!" he exclaimed. "Everything suits you, Honey!" he further continued.

"Well! Then I'll go with pink only" I confirmed with a smirk.

(As I already selected red in my mind)

"You know Tasha – the Queen – you have already selected your desired shade but still you asked me" he groaned in irritation. "You girls shop according to your own wish and mood. It's useless of asking to a boy to help you girls out for shopping. As you select what you like rather than what you partner prefers for you…huh" he answered angrily.

"Hahaha" I made an evil laugh.

Samir interrupted, "Sweetie…I'll call you back in ten minutes. Have some work."

"Alright" I replied than disconnected the call.

I plugged the earphone, selected my favorite song on my playlist and started dancing on the tunes. Oops not dancing actually jumping on the couch.

One song, two song, three, four, five till I reach the twelfth song. I peered at the watch, Samir said he'll call me in ten minutes but already more than twenty- five have passed on.

Let me call him, and remind him – that he has a girlfriend.

I abruptly dialed his number. He attended my call.

And

Suddenly I heard a loud sound as if something has crashed down. The cacophonous noise echoed through the darkness. The sound seemed too unpleasant, I felt as if it was hammering my ear. While listening to the discordant sound suddenly I felt as if my throat chocked up, was not able to gulp up my own saliva. Fear captured my body with variety of weird wrong thoughts flying in my mind.

Could not figure out what was going on, on the other side of the phone. I said, "Samir are you there, are you listening to my voice."

After few seconds, I peered at my cell phone and found out that the call got disconnected. All the wrong thoughts captured my mind. The only thought that submerges in the ocean of my mind was that, "Samir must be fine."

In hesitation manner I dialed the number again.

It's ringing…once twice thrice and further it went on ringing.

Pick up, pick up, pick up…I pleaded quietly.

I called back again…this time the call was answered.

From the other side of the call, "Hmm" was stated. While hearing the voice a sign of relief was felt in the pit of my stomach. My body muscles relaxed while I adjusted myself back on the sofa.

I said, "Samir are you alright?"

No answer.

I repeated, "Samir can you hear me?"

No answer.

Please!!!!! Say something. I said once, twice, thrice but no answer. I was curious and could not understand what was wrong and kept on saying Samir can u hear me, in spite of my repeated efforts no answer was received. And the phone got disconnected.

I kept on dialing the number, a number of times but no one was answering. It is such times, one often find mobile battery low.

"Ehh…warning flashed on the screen – "*Battery low – connect to the charger*"

I plugged to the charger and waited near the phone only.

After half an hour my phone rang, I received the call from Samir's number; I felt as if my wish came true, I answered the call immediately without thinking anything. I said, "Where were you, why were you not answering my call."

On the other side of the phone someone answered, "Madam, I am a police officer. Mr. Samir has met with an accident and we are taking him to the nearest City Hospital."

After delivering the news of the accident from the police officer, I broke down completely and the phone slide from my hand on the ground.

It was a shock to my ears; my body did not understand how to react. Mouth slightly open; body unmoving and color started draining from my face. Eyes widen staring in one direction. My body froze up to one point where I was finding difficulty in breathing.

It is sometimes difficult to express how you undergo in an unexpected situation. I had no words to speak, all of a sudden I felt that my body was been caught by paralysis. I was stunned by hearing this news as could not believe what my ears have heard.

Jiya my younger sister happen to enter my room, she saw tears were rolling down my cheeks and my body was shivering. Jiya kept on asking, what happen?

I answered, in a low and a cracking voice, it seemed as if I was struggling to speak, I said "He met wit a car acci… dent, I broke down completely."

My phone which was laying dead on the floor had a continuous echo coming from it, "Madam, are you there."

While observing that, Jiya happen to attend the call and answered, "Hello." The rest story the police officer narrated to her. After knowing the news Jiya was also in a distress state, but soon she collected her senses and came back to the material world.

Jiya fumbled in her speech, "Tasha lets rush to the City Hospital."

I could her voice but I was unable to react. Felt as if my body was as stiff as a rock, my legs where embedded in the earth. Jiya catch hold my hand and dragged me out towards our car in the parking space.

We entered the hospital quickly, started gathering the information from the hospital staff about Samir, one of the nurse informed that he has been shifted to the operation theatre.

The nurse claimed that the patient was badly injured, the face was enclosed by wounds, and body was wet with blood. Their were deep cuts all over his body occurring due to accident with excessive blood flowing out of his body.

I, Jiya and Samir's mom dad were waiting outside the operation theatre and continuously chanting prayers, hoping for a miracle to occur and save Samir.

Roughly after 3 hours operation was over. Doctors and nurses came out of the operation theatre; we all rushed towards the doctors and quietly we were starring at the doctor.

Our heart beats were thumping fast, waiting for the doctor to say something. In a low and firm voice he addressed, "I am sorry, we could not save him". It was hard to believe the bitter truth, which nobody was able to swallow.

My brows furrowed with disbelief and eyes flooded with water. Tears coming out of my eyes making my vision blur. I never thought god would be so brutal and cruel towards me.

The doctor said "that the last we understood was he exclaimed in a firm voice was Tasha".

The police officer named Inspector Rajeev Kandal was standing next to the doctor. Fetching out; all the possible information relating to the accident. He further suggested the doctor to hand over the postmortem report as soon as possible so that he can carry out his further investigation.

After completing a long conversation with the doctor, Inspector Rajeev headed towards Samir's Dad to gather further information relating to the whole scene. Samir's Dad passed on all essential details but seemed that Inspector was not contented with the accident scene.

Further he walked towards Samir's Mom to know more about the situation but he could not get any answer from her as she was crying out loudly in agony.

After getting dishearten, he walked towards me to know the whole story of Samir in hope that he might get some clue of the occurrence of the accident. He approached me and Jiya stating, "Can I talk to you people for a while."

After wiping our tears, I and Jiya nodded our heads. Jiya said in a low tone, "Yes please, how can we help you?"

Inspector Rajeev further stated in a question mark expression, "Can you tell me where Samir was going tonight?"

Jiya was about to answer in the mean time I interrupted controlling all my emotions, "That tonight; Samir had gone out with his friends for parting in a pub. It was his close friend birthday blast. The only problem was that he will never ever return home. Leaving me and his family all alone in dark."

The only thought that had been running through my mind was that I would never be able to see him again. No more teasing, no more dinners, no more movies and the worst of all, no more love and lovely kisses from the most important person in my life.

Inspector Rajeev made some frown lines on his forehead and in a suspicious way said, "Strange none of his friends are present in the hospital." At listening to this sentence even I had a doubt but later realized that none might be aware that Samir met with an accident.

Jiya interrupted in between my thoughts and said to the inspector and me, "Might be Samir's friend must have all left and after that Samir met with the accident."

Inspector responded, "Might be this all must be true and I am suspecting to much, but on the accident spot I found some pieces of rare unshaped greenish-blue stones broken sleeping on the ground." Placing those stones in his hand he showed them to us.

"Do you people recognize them", he stately abruptly. We both looked at those unshaped mat finishing stone and nodded in disbelief. I shrugged my shoulder and said, "We have never seen these stones before today."

Listening this much, Inspector Rajeev opened in a file which was named as "Hit and Drive Cases" and entered Samir's Name in that file after that turned his back and started moving in the opposite direction. Hospital staff hands over Samir's body and belonging to us.

The funeral was something that was captured in my mind for the rest of my life, making me feel completely helpless in saving him. The entire ceremony consisted of relatives along with long chain of tears and condolences making me feel more depressed and lonely.

After the funeral I stopped going anywhere. Except often used to visit places where I and Samir often used to spend quality time, & was quite regular to his restaurants for managing it.

It felt as if the earth stopped to rotate, the clock did not move. There was no life existing in me. There was numbness throughout my body. Depression state which was not under my control. It was an emotional breakdown which was slowly and gradually capturing me.

After sobbing for what seemed to be months, one day I decided and collected all the belongings including his gifts, greeting cards and all the stuffs of Samir which I had as his remembrance and placed them into a bag. I zipped close the bag and kept them in a dark room of my apartment and decided never to visit them again.

I tried to never think of Samir but it pained me to know that his absence would continue for the rest of my life.

Did not even realize when the days started converting into months and months into years but for me the sad season did not change. The fog blocked the sun to rise from the horizon making it appear blur.

New Beginning

Returning from the flashback, the next day.

It was approximately 8.30 am on the busy morning. Meeting was fixed with the bank managers. Hoping I could extend some time for repayment of loan.

I couldn't focus on anything else. Nothing. Nothing except the feeling of the familiar crystal-clear black eyes of Samir gazing at me. His eyes made me feel as if they are speaking "to protect my dream, to protect my family restaurants".

Somehow somewhere it felt as if Samir was standing next to me. Giving me hope and courage to fight with this situation.

Waiting for Samir's Dad. It was necessary for both of us to be present for the meeting with the bank managers. Samir's Dad carried a lot of reputation and I was a bit sure, that he would be able to influence the bank manager for loan extension.

After Samir's death, he never paid any attention towards the restaurant business. He often used to sit alone in the room for hours and look intently at Samir's photo.

Emptiness and sorrow encircled him. The grief holds him all stiff, not allowing him to come out of the pain.

In the meantime while I was impatiently waiting for him, I received a call from Kabir. I answered the call instantly, "Damn you kabira. Where have you been since these days?" I whined. "Wish me luck, hope today the day turns for me into a ray of hope. All it is you can pray for me."

"CEASE…my friend. God is always with his devotees" he answered.

"Ohh…God… yeah" I winked while holding all the restaurant and banks papers in my hand. Kabir being a true believer in god. While me having a constant fight with god. Irony one is a great believer and the other is a fearless fighter. Heard the noise of car, I frequently interrupted, "Will get back to you soon, Uncle arrived."

Uncle arrived and I was all set to go for the meeting, I headed towards his car. I greeted, "hello uncle, how are you"

He replied, in his painful voice, "I am fine. How are you this morning?"

We both were hiding our unhappiness from each other. I answered, "Me too fine".

I heard the door of the car opening behind me and I turned around to see who was it?

The door opened, a tall man came out, dressed in a black suit, white shirt, and black tie that hugged his body. He had very well built body and broad shoulders. The body was toned properly, seemed that the person regularly knocks the gym.

His brown eyes were captivating and created charm in his personality. His black hair was a little bit longer which just added more to his attractiveness.

I pulled myself out of this little paradise his looks were taking me into and decided to figure out the reason of an unexpected visit of a complete stranger.

I turned towards Uncle, and observing at my confused face and having an internal debate, he replied with a smile, "Meet Mr. Ayan, he is accompanying us in the meeting".

Ayan extended his right hand towards me, pointing his thumb upward and exclaimed "hello Tasha". In fraction of second even, I extended my right hand towards him for a handshake and said, "hello Ayan, how you doing?"

Followed by words, "welcome to family, great to have you with us".

He in turn answered, "I am glad, thank you" followed with a smile or either a grin, hiding some expression in that smile.

We all settled in the car. Uncle and Ayan occupied the front seat; I occupied the back passenger seat. All were set to go for the meeting.

Throughout the road journey, I kept myself calm and quiet, felt as if having a battle with my inner soul.

Trains of thought were running in mind, it made me feel incomplete in Samir's Dad eyes. He must be thinking that I am not capable of handling the burden of restaurant business.

Of course I did not prove myself in bring the restaurant business back on track. So many thoughts were waving in my mind.

I felt a need to speak to uncle, is it safe to disclose our financial details to an outsider?

But I could not gather enough courage to open my mouth and speak like that. As I was aware that whatever decision he would take, would in return turn out to be fruitful for our business.

So I decided to maintain peace with my inner soul.

Uncle and Ayan were having conversation with each other. While talking to Ayan, uncle had a sweet and innocent smile on his face. After years, I saw him smiling with someone.

Could make out from his face, how badly he must be missing his young son. But he never showed his deep emotion to anyone. Quietly he used to gulp down this distress.

As after Samir's death, his Mom entered into the world of depression.

So to keep her healthy and happy, he used hide his sufferings form all.

Watching his smile, my eyes went wet and I was about to cry, but somehow I tried to hold my sentiment and shattered my thoughts outside the window of the car and tried to pay attention on their conversation.

Uncle laughed and said loudly Tasha, "he is not stranger to us anymore. Ayan and Samir are childhood friends. Our families know each other very well since years. Often we people have family get – together. Our families try to meet once in a year.

By hearing this I was a bit astonished, as I had never heard about Ayan from the horses mouth, I mean from Samir's mouth.

He claimed, "Samir and Ayan completed there studies in the same university. They both proceeded for their hotel management in the same year from London University.

He has opened chains of Indian restaurant in London. Created huge revolution in the food business with fancy yet affordable restaurants springing all over the city. With an influx of barbecue grills, burgers, Indian cuisine and quirky dinners that combine the likes of sparkling wine and hot dogs, the rumble in fancy yet affordable alternative for eating out is clear."

While uncle portrayed a detailed description of Ayan, I happen to glared at him. I glared at him because; I was a bit uncomfortable by his presence. Actually I turned into a ball of fire still I tired to content my anger.

As for these restaurants was the greatest priority of Samir, and being frank I did not want any unknown person to administer it. These restaurants made me think of him.

"It was not the feeling of completeness which I would feel in the restaurant, which I so needed but it did not make me feel empty".

Inside of the restaurant reminded the time when I Samir used to giggle around and manage the customers and staff entering our heaven place i.e. our restaurant. This wasn't less than a heaven for us.

We used to make sure our customers would receive royal treatment and lavishly served dishes and sweets and while leaving their stomach should be filed and their pants get a bit tighten.

I already stepped in the ocean of my own thoughts; suddenly a car in front of our car slides close to our car. And, uncle happen to apply a sudden break due to which a strong jerk was felt by us. Due to the jerk we all in the car moved frequently forward and instantly back to our original position.

Thanks to the car manufacturers who make seat belts for safety. As the seat beats were embedded through uncle and Ayan's body, they did not hurt themselves. While this jerk did not hurt me out either, only it helped me to move out of my waves of thoughts and made me realize I was sitting in the car with two gentlemen.

While I looked at Ayan through the mirror inside the car to give him a gesture of smile.

I discover on my surprise that he was constantly gazing at me. His intense brown eyes were constantly viewing me.

It made me feel his eyes were speaking something, some words they were trying to depict; some truth was behind his eyes made my thought process rotate faster.

His intense eyes were captivating me.

This sought of non-verbal communication between us, in which we both looked at each other's eye at same time made me more of uncomfortable in the car.

The Meeting Turning Fruitfully

*A*yan came all prepared for the meeting. He collected all data, graphs and possible every diagrams and different trends of various restaurants which were necessary for convincing the managers.

He even collected all the past data of our company and showed our progress rate too. He made assurance that the restaurants will be back in the market with a bang. He insured that the banks will soon get there regular loan installments with the desired rate of interest.

The last word which he painted to them was, "to have faith in us for the last time, after that they can proceed with acquiring the property and disposing it off".

After his speech, there was a pause for a long time, the managers where discussing among themselves, they scanned all the possible details available and given by Ayan and discussed twice, thrice and so on.

Finally it was a sign of relief, for me and uncle, that bank managers were taking keen interests on the words delivered by Ayan.

A smile appeared on my face, and I was grateful to Ayan, that at least he tried his level best to defend the restaurants.

Meeting turned out to be fertile. Bank managers agreed with his terms. Placing some of there own do's and don'ts, which was accepted by all of us. Joy overrides are stressful emotions. A tear rolled down my cheek but even a smile appeared on my face at the same time.

Some of the bank managers left and some where sitting in the conference room, uncle left towards the parking lot. In the mean time I and Ayan were collecting and shuffling all the documents. Within no time, I sighed, "Thanks Ayan, I appreciate all your hard works and efforts towards the restaurants".

He smiled, and retorted while looking deep inside my eyes, "I'll be always there for you, Honey".

I answered instantly, "what?"

By hearing this, I frowned over him. Before I could demand an explanation.

His eyes rolled down towards the papers, shuffling the shuffled papers. Although everything he was doing at the moment contradicted his line.

Collecting all the papers, uplifting the papers towards my squint eyes, he exclaimed, "I'll be always there for you, the papers".

It felt, "Ahhhh…awful."

I started to leave. He shouted "Miss Princess, please carry thy (your) papers with you."

I winked at him carrying a lot of attitude, "I know I am, princess. So I'll not carry that load."

Ayan gave me a blank stare.

"I am thy (your) Princess, so thee (you) servant…carry those papers with you." I responded with a proud smirk on my face.

He within a fraction of seconds went on his knees bowed down and said, "Your highness…at your service."

"What the hell is he doing? I muttered to myself having a pit of embarrassment forming on my face as some officers inside the room were peering at us. I felt as if there was no use of demanding an explanation from him. His attitude started rubbing me and making me more annoyed. It suddenly became hard for me to swallow those words, while I hesitated before questioning him more.

I hastily walked towards and snatched the papers form his hands while placing them into my bag without even zipping it up. And ran straight towards the door. Pulling the door – instead it was written push the door – hitting the handle of the door out of frustration - where carrying the most awkward expression on my face.

Ayan standing extremely back of me, while his chest touched to my back. His body touches, were sending sparks to me. He placed his face extremely on my left shoulder and utter in my left ear, making some of my hair strands flew a bit high through the words he spoke, "Allow me, Princess."

My eyes rolled left side to peer at him. While his eyes were already at his right side, glancing at me with a smirk on his face. His eyes were captivating. He placed his hand on my hand which was rested on the handle and pushed the door. A thunder storm struck my body due to his touch.

For half a moment we both peered in each others eyes and forgot the world.

A loud sound from the back interrupted, "Excuse us please" made us come back to reality. Our eye contact ceased while I walked out from the door.

I decided better to continue with the work. His gestures were annoying me but still I was thankful towards him as he was able to conquer the loan extension.

While returning home, uncle requested me to take Ayan along as a guest at my place. Initially I hesitated but after uncle's couples of request forced me to agree with him. As I was aware about Samir's Mom mental condition, the only solution left with me was to take him with me.

I glanced at him. He was leaning towards the car – obviously waiting for my answer.

"WELCOME… home" I gave him a death glare. I must confess his eyes carried a lot of naughtiness. Again, I was immersed into them – God there were incredible.

He smirked.

And I got my answer, troubles on my way to home - I mean, I only invited the trouble – Gosh, its gonna be tough – I could sense it.

There were three things I was certain about.

1.   Ayan would be staying with us – and off course I had to bear him.
2.   My room would be offered to him as the guest room.

And the final one was…

3.   He would be staying here for long.

Ehhhhhh!!! My face made those entire irritating emoticon in my mind. ;- (: - <

Ting Tong I rang the door bell.

Jiya opened the door. Before giving me smile, she preferred to stare at Ayan.

Like, really staring at him…

I snap my fingers and made sound while twisting my fingers to bring her back to earth.

"AHH… Jiya mumbled.

"Now will you just excuse, so that we can get inside." I replied with frustration.

Ayan interrupted, "Yes, please– just excuse here – she is a bit fat soooooo – or else she will get struck at the door."

At this definitely Jiya giggled. While I gazed at Ayan with full of anger and answered, "You mean that – I'm fat – joke of the day….HA HA HA"

He looked at my body, full from up and down and grinned.

"Typical boyish behavior" I groaned not that loud but it was audible for him.

He walked close to me. Very close to me, the gap between us was totally vanished. I could hear his breathes + my breathe multiplying twice the speed. Peered in my eyes and shouted, "You at least need to lose 2 kg" and laughed out loud.

"Whatever" I whimpered and left towards my room.

Jiya and Ayan in no time gel well with each other. Ayan introduced himself to Mom. And in no time Ayan adjusted well in the family.

I stripped my office clothes and made myself comfortable in shorts and a loose top while cleaning the room for Ayan. Rushing down I claimed, "The room is ready, make yourself comfortable."

While he said bye to Jiya, and walked towards the staircase dragging his bag. I muttered softly waiting for him at the staircase so that only he could hear, "Beware of my room – don't mess it – or else ghost will be all around."

He winked his eyes in astonishment and whimper, "Dare to the Ghost – I'll be waitingggggggg……"

-------------------------* * * * * * *-------------------------

Mission----Blue Diary

Mom and Jiya did not utter a word, just blankly staring at me. I understood the atmosphere was tensed and they were eager to know the results of the meeting. A bit of naughtiness grabbed my mind, so pretended and made saddy faces so could manage to create the most threatening atmosphere, within few seconds Mom and Jiya were finding it hard to breathe.

Looking at there tensed face, my small laughter broke out. Seeing my laughter everyone at my place realize that the meeting turned out successful. I explained every single moment of the meeting to Mom and Jiya. They were happy with our first step towards our success.

After completing our dinner, a while later, as I laid down on the mattress in the Jiya's room and looked outside the window, I saw the full moon shinning hanging high up in the sky. I got up straight from my bed and sat near the window & another beautiful scene I witnessed was the moon appeared like a pearl down on the wrinkling water in the lake near to my house and it looked absolutely amazing. A smile was plastered on my face.

Snuggling into my blanket with a smile on my face, I kept wondering "maybe this will be a new start for the restaurants and for all".

Before my brain started to shut down and my eyes closed, the thought of the blue diary awestruck me to read further the poems and quotes. Some where the diary made me feel cozy and tranquil while reading it.

God!!! My search engine started to dig the diary but I guess I left it in my room. Now as I shifted in Jiya's room.

My heart began to drum against my chest, my breathe running fast. I need that diary thought it was not my possession still I needed. Thought for a while – tried to sleep – various ideas hit my mind – but all seemed impossible.

That's it…I decided - I guess - I need to break in my own house and that to in my own room.

I opened Jiya's room door and headed towards my room. Unfortunately for the time being it was Ayan's room. I tried several times to unlock the door but it was closed. All my hard work was going in vain.

Pulling # pushing # hitting # kicking # etc etc…but the door did not open. I muttered to myself, "Silly doors… for the first time I felt…why god made locks on the doors."

Waiting outside the room I prayed to God, please give me some idea to drop in.

Please…. Please…. Please….

It was as if my wish comes true. Suddenly the knob of the door was twisted and the door opened. Before Ayan could come out I flipped to the side wall and hide myself behind his back without being noticed by him.

Felt as if I was a thief in my own house. Awwwww!!!

Like it happens in the movie some one comes out from the room -and you happen to hide behind the person - and slowly you move inside the room.

Same was my case…………

Ayan was half in sleep. I guess because of my prolong pressing the knob his sleep might have got disturbed.

Finally I was in my room hiding behind the door. Honestly, I don't think I have ever prayed so much in my entire life. My eyes were shut and I constantly kept on praying in my heart.

God, please don't wake him up…
God, please don't wake him up…
God, please don't wake him up…

He shut the door while yawning he jumped on the bed. Slowly I opened my eyes to view the scene.

My heart drops down from my chest seeing my room being so messy. I felt to kick him on his butt and throw him down from the bed in anger.

I muttered to myself, "now, how the hell…I'll search the diary in such a messy room?"

I glanced at Ayan and a sweet smile made its way on my face seeing him sleepy. He looked so innocent like a baby while sleeping.

"FOCUS" my mind ordered me.

Only two things I need to focus at the moment.

1.   Search and grab the blue diary.
2.   Leave fast before he gets up.

While I started to look around for the blue diary without making any noise – it took almost five minutes for me to realize – that the diary was lying under Ayan's head.

Questions - 1- Now what?

2 - Am I dead?

3 - No rescue plan?

4 - What the hell I'll do if he wakes up?

Answers - Might be I'll say sorry or may be sing a lullaby. Silly I'll just hit the book on his head strongly so that he becomes unconscious and goes deep in sleep.

It was beginning to sound like some cartoon movie. Where hitting a book on head can make cartoon characters unconscious and suddenly the birds starts flying around the head.

God…Ayan was snoring so loud that one can make out that he is deep in his dreams. So might as well I can give it a try and drag the diary and go out.

But of all it was decided that I need the diary. So finally I decided to shift Ayan's head slightly and pull the book beneath his head and grab and go.

I walked towards the bed. Leaned towards him and slowly started trying to lift his head in the meantime dragging the book out from his head.

Suddenly, my hand was seized and he shouted in his sleepy voice, "Thief !!! Thief !!! Thief !!!…

"Shhhhh….." I painted in a low voice while my eyes widening over his creepiness.

Being my wrist caught tight by him - nor could I go and switch on the tube light - nor could shut his mouth.

He lifted himself up from the bed and dragged me towards the wall. My back attached to the wall and both the hands were caught hold tight by him while his chest affix to mine.

And finally the curtain flew due to the cool breeze moving making the moon's light hit on our faces making our face visible to each other.

My eyes were closed due to the fear of his closeness and breathes were heavy. His grip was tight enough not allowing me to move.

SILENCE... no noise at all. I gathered all my courage to open one of my eyes and see. I saw a flash of amusement in his eyes right when his lips formed into a smirk.

"Miss Princess, what made you Miss Thief tonight?
Or
Were you like checking me out at midnight? He painted.

"Nothing" I answered and starting struggling to get out of his hold.

He tightens his grip on my hands while pushed his face close to mine and uttered, "Either give me an answer or stay like that for the whole night - choice is yours babes".

Well, his closeness was sending sparks in my body. I kept struggling to get off from his grip. The more I tried the more he would tighten his grip.

Finally, I gave up. I need that diary which was lying beneath your head.

"Ehh!!! For that diary you became a thief tonight" he mumbled.

"So can I take the diary back and go" I answered in an irritating tone.

"Now if you want to go - than you should say SORRY to me - and than say PLEASE" the monster replied with the smirk on his face.

Without hesitating I at once said both the words one after the other.

"Princess, please be soft and polite before saying" he muttered with his famous smirk.

If felt as if the monster was like a giant brick wall. He would not agree so soon. So at the end, I had to let my defenses go down and say it softly and in a polite manner.

"Now can I go" I hummed in displeasure.

"No…" he winked.

"Monster" I spurted out loudly.

His eyes widened at the word while forming the smirk on his face. "Well, now I'll not let you go so easily".

After hearing this I started to struggle even more to escape. But this time he tightens his hold more and stretched both my arms widely attached to the walls. He was even closer than before. I could hear his heartbeat while he could count my heartbeats.

"Now, you need to sing, a song before you leave" he uttered making his breathe touch my face.

"Ohh shit…I am a bad singer" I replied.

"Damn…good!!! Now you need to sing for sure" he answered carrying naughtiness in his voice.

My eyes blinked at his stupidity.

"No" I spurt out loud.

He winked stating, "Choice is yours – either sing – or – stay locked her for the whole night".

"Ahhh…" I shouted. Was aware he was a solid brick wall. Would agree only on his, own terms and condition. This is the only reason even the bank managers got convinced with his proposals.

"You're kidding me right?" I asked giving him a death glare.

"WELL…sing or stay. Choice is your babes" he painted his sexy soft voice into my ear.

Suddenly, noises of the footsteps were audible. Probably, Mom would be awake as Ayan shouted, "**THIEF THIEF THIEF**". Her sleep must have got disturbed due to his screaming.

"LEAVE…I suppose mom is coming" I uttered in a begging tone while struggle to move from his grip.

"Not that easy. Sing and go or else I'll say your Mom?" he said in his sexy tone.

"Say what?" I mumbled with complete blank expression.

"Firstly -----

You at midnight –

In the moonlight – he winked.

All alone –

In my room –

With a sexy young boy" he replied while forming a cunning smirk on his face.

After hearing this eyes turned wet. Single tear made its own road ways to come down all through my cheek. Could not understand what shall I do? In the meantime I noticed Ayan and was astonish to see him.

Ayan loosens a bit – his grip on my hand was almost gone – he made a wide gap between us – making way for me.

"Aww…please don't cry. I can't see any one crying" he painted having some guilt on his face.

"Bingooooo…I guess I made the boy - having a strong muscular body – weak." I muttered to myself. It was at this time I realized tears at times are useful or you can even say works as weapons helping to win over your enemy.

Making the best use of the chance -Slightly I slide across him – grabbed the book from the bed – walked towards the door.

The excitement wasn't yet over.

I was about to open the door. Suddenly a knock was placed on the door and Mom happened to open the door. I flipped back sideways with the door and hide myself behind the door.

Mom entered and said, "Is everything alright? I suppose you screamed?" In the meantime I was hiding behind the door and praying to god.

"Nothing Aunty - just saw a big sexy ghost in my dreams – now it's gone – don't get bother." He hummed.

"GHOST….ehhh…referring to me – how dare he?" I whimpered to myself in aggression while keeping my eyes closed and continuous praying to god.

Mom answered, "Hmmm……GHOST" taking a long pause she again mumbled, "Sure everything alright."

"YES" he winked.

"Goodnight…sleep well" mom answered and shut the door and left.

"HUH…" a sign of relief painted in my breathe as she left from the room.

I unlocked my eyelashes and peered at Ayan, who still had a smirk lingered on his lips.

"GHOSTTTTT…. WHATEVER……." I answered with anger and left the room after finding it safe.

--------------MISSION ACCOMPLISH ----------BLUE DIARY --------------

I opened some random page, page 42 it stated,

INSPIRATION

**My words, my thoughts, my soul
It is the inspiration that rolls.**

**My strength, my mind, my heart
It is the inspiration that will never apart.**

After reading those lines, I don't even realize when I wrapped the blue diary with my arms, hugged it tightly to my chest and not knowing when my eyes were shut down taking me into the new world of dreams.

Waking up the next morning, my eyes were immediately affected by the sun shining into my room as I completely forgotten to close the curtains night before going to sleep as being unaware when I was lost into my dreams.

Frankly speaking, the sun wasn't definitely something that I enjoyed seeing first thing in the morning. But after years I felt that the fog got separated and the sun made its own way to rise from the horizon.

Rolling over in my bed, cuddling further into the warmth of my blanket, as a feeling of happiness flowed through my body I folded my hands while closing my eyes prayed to God to turn this day into a bright ray of hope. After my prayers I opened my eyes and viewed on my bedside clock which currently showed me the numbers that it was quarter to seven making me realize I would be late to the restaurant and rushing to get ready and arrive at the restaurant before Ayan would reach.

After taking a quick shower, brushing my teeth and moving my hair dryer for a couple of minutes on my wet hair. I was now searching my clothes hanging in my closet.

After having a battle with my inner self and getting jumbled with the question of what to wear and what not to wear, actually getting confused as I and Ayan were meeting up in the restaurant basically to clean it up, to change its interior to do some touch up on the walls etc.

Finally I grabbed out a pair of denim shorts and a comfortable tank top out from the hangers and draped them on me. Along with applying a little mascara onto my eyelashes with a bit of lip balm and keeping my hair open before leaving my premises and heading towards the restaurant.

Greeted my mom and requested her to send Ayan directly to the restaurant.

Reality Hits On The Face

I entered the restaurant early by 8.00am.Wanted to give a fresh start to the new era of my enthusiasm.

A few seconds later, Ayan entered. He was wearing jet black color pants with a luscious lemon shirt hugged to his chest that was slightly unbuttoned at the collar.

"Hey" I greeted, standing to his left side to let him in.

"Hi" he looked around my restaurant as he came in for some odd reason, I was nervous about what he might have been thinking about it.

It felt like he was judging me and the place.

"Make yourself comfortable. Would you like anything to drink?" I said while heading towards the kitchen. "No thanks" he replied as he sat on one of the chair.

He quickly viewed all the corners of the restaurant. Making some rough calculations in his mind. Hastily dialed some numbers and ordered something. From the kitchen I tried to understand what his further plans were. But could not figure out what he was up to.

In meantime he entered the kitchen; his search engine was on, basically his eyes were searching something to eat. He was going to and fro like a pendulum in the kitchen. His moving disturbed me and annoyed too. I stopped my work and with a bit of irritating voice I asked "what do you need?"

He replied, turning the bottle of coffee round and round and tossing the bottle up in air "this my love". His flirtatious line made me feel to punch him hard. My back was facing him; I turned towards him and was about to throw the ball of fire of words on his head.

Suddenly I saw few people entering the restaurant with carrying huge boxes and wires in their hand.

They placed the boxes in front of us, and Ayan quickly checked their bills and paid them off.

"What are these boxes and wires for?" I asked hastily. He did not even bother to answer any of my questions and the very next few minutes he started unpacking the pile of boxes and making sure everything he had ordered has arrived here safely.

I repeatedly kept on asking the same question, "What you are up to, can you please explain?" I followed him from one place to another. He kept moving forward and carried on with his work, I was just standing behind his back with full of anger and he happened to turn around and moved towards me, within no time I lost my control and would fell into on one of those boxes and wires, so I tried to hold Ayan's luscious lemon yellow color shirt's collar during the fall so that I could become stable and get my balance back, in the mean time Ayan even lost his control and he followed my fall. Ayan was holding certain number of pages in hands, due to the fall the papers flew high up in the air and coming down one by one. Some papers flew here and there and some papers coming on our heads.

The boxes on which we both fell contain paints and one of the paint bottle bursts out, within a fraction of seconds the red color splashed all over us. Ayan seized me tightly from the waist while flipped over me and began to rotate on the floor as many boxes began to burst out due to our heavy weight in the mean time we both were getting tied up with wires due to our constant rotating. Within no time our fair complexion turned into color red. Red color was over our body and covered our face too making us wet in red with the wires locked around our whole body.

My body had stiffened at Ayan's proximity.

I drifted to get up; his hands were around my wet waist securely wrapped around me, burning flames and sparks into me. I mentally shook my head and began to pull away. I struggled a number of times to drift myself form the warmth of his body but could not succeed as the paint every time made my attempt fail. The paint made me and him slip over and over. Making me hold him tighter than before.

Every time I attempted to drift myself, he would tighten his grip from my back. In the intervening time he just peered at me with an innocent smile. I just glanced at him once in a disgusting way and mumbled in an irritating voice, "Will you stop staring at me and get up so that your heavy weight drifts up from my body. And I can even get up."

After also saying in such a rude tone all Ayan could do was just staring without even blinking his eyes even once and constantly displaying a childlike smile on his lips. All I could do is shake his shoulders and wake him up and bring him back to the planet.

While forming his famous smirk he said, "No."

"Eww…you weigh like a hundred tones, get up" I replied in the most disgusting way.

"No, before that you need to allow me something." He replied in the most genuine tone.

"What to allow?" I answered in confused state.

He uttered in a soft voice, "There are certain wires which have rolled around your neck, so please allow me to pick it up or else once you try to get up your neck will be tied up by the wires making you feel suffocated."

I stared at him blankly; he wasn't serious, was he?

"Please allow me" he muttered in his decent voice.

"Err…no" I offended.

"Tasha, please understand" he responded.

"Noooooo…." Peered in his eyes for the moment and replied with firm determination.

"Please listen calmly" he insisted.

I just had the worst expression on my face.

"Listen…we both are wet and unable to get up as all wires have tied us all together. There may be failure of attempts to lift our self's. During those attempts you might get hurt from those wires." He made me understand in the simplest manner.

I utter to myself, is there any other way left out? – shall I allow him? – How will he lift up the wires? – We both are locked all around with wires + paint spread all around our body.

My brain answered me, wait a minute. This part of my life is called, "having no other choice."

"Fine..." I stated with no expression.

His eyes blinked in amusement.

I rested my body down completely on the floor while my hands still wrapped around his neck and his hands locked behind my waist while my eyes peering at his actions. As he said he'll close his eyes slowly, softly bends his head down towards my neck

His lips crash down my neck's skin making my breathe run fast while automatically making my eyes shut down. His lips rubbed here and there struggling hard to catch hold the wires from his lips. My breathe increasing manifold times as and when his attempts fail to pick the wire. Every time his lips brush my skin it would light thousands of sparks into me.

Finally he caught hold of the wire and lifted himself with the wire locked between his lips. I peered at his innocent face with the eyes closed till yet. At witnessing this scene, my lips automatically formed the curve line making me smile.

He slowly opened his eyes and peered at me.

"Now, will you please get up" I stated.

"Wait, for a minute, I'll help you in getting up." He whispered. Slowly he struggled to make both of us stand up. My hands were folded behind his neck.

He uttered, "Your almond shape eyes are gorgeous. Anyone can go crazy for them". These lines made my eyes grow larger followed by a small smile.

Within a short time, we were able to drift our self. We unfolded our hands from each others body and unlocking the wires tied up all around us. After getting release from the wires I started to move from his glaze, he said loudly 'Tasha,

**"In life you have to walk alone for a while,
The distance might convert into miles.
To overcome the distance it is worth to smile,
The first step to overcome sadness is to smile,
The last step to finish sadness is also smile.
Only the distance in between is remaining
Walk for some miles, the path will unravel itself
Making you smile worthwhile."**

Followed by further words, "You only live once, so live your life to the fullest. God never said that life will be fair, but he gave as the ability to make it fine." After hearing those words I felt the limbs of my body quivering and mouth drying up, was stunned and was at a stand still mode.

After few seconds I gathered my attention, turned around without even bothering to answer him and started zipping my bag.

The only thing hitting my head was Ayan had no right to interfere in my personal life. He is not at all aware about my life's journey, so who the hell gave him the right to judge me. He is all here to help the restaurant to survive rather not here to help me out to come out of my pain.

The only few objects occupying my head was Love – Samir – Anger – Ayan – Happiness – Samir – Hurt – Ayan – Past – Samir – Present – Ayan – Confusion – Samir/ Ayan – Finalllly….Frustration & Hate – Mr. Ayan.

God dammit, I started collecting all my belongings and rolling my hair round in a bun, carried my bag and walked towards the exit of the restaurant.

"Tasha!"

Silence…I did not answer.

"Tasha…Tasha!"

I started running fast to get rid of this so called paranoid boy. What ever action he would do would contradict his personality. He was just "Uggh…..Creepy."

"Tasha listen" he was just beside me now, to get my attention he slightly hit me on my arm.

I could do was just ignore and walk fast.

"God dammit…just hold on for a second. Why aren't you replying to me?"

I really did not bother to answer him again.

And this ignorance was the last which I could do. Before I could walk towards my car, Ayan stepped in front of me to get an answer.

"Move Ayan" I demanded.

"Woah…Woah…are you getting angry?" he asked while rubbing his handkerchief on his wet paint face.

"Yes, now get aside." I tried to step to my right while he shifted to his left soon as to block my way.

"Why are you angry at me???" he stated in a firm voice.

This time my anger reached its maximum point, without even thinking further I yelled at him, "I am not here to answer any of your questions."

"Umm…I understood...you can't seriously be mad at me because I was just making you love your life again" he explained with a bit of frustration.

"You are Mr. Nobody, and you have no rights to interfere in my life. Whatever I am… However I am…I am perfect for myself."

"Are you insane? I am not interfering in your life. Just saying you to love your life again – saying to take chance again – saying to live again – saying to believe in miracles – saying to love again – saying to maintain peace with your past" he screamed.

I looked at him straight in the eyes, carrying all the power in my voice for the moment and stated, "You are here for uplifting the restaurant not for uplifting my life. Better just carry on with that work only" and than I just walked away.

Silence was spread all around.

After our last encounter, Ayan did not stop me.

But all he made me realize that I forgot to smile. I forgot to live. I forgot to love. What I did not forget was, I did not forget to shed tears.

I felt as if reality is hitting on my face.

_____XXX_____

AYAN'S WORDS

At times I wish god must give every individual certain powers where one can see the future and can change themselves accordingly – only for the sake of others happiness.

For the past one hour, ten minutes and twenty-two seconds Tasha left, all I could recollect was her sad but astonished face. I guess I should have not crossed my limits. Her actions did not hurt me rather than those words – and more than her words her silence will kill me more now.

I guess what hurt most will be the fact that just when I was willing to be a part of her live – it is exactly this point when she will neglect me – this pain will be butchery me form within.

I just removed the cigarette packet from my pocket and lit one of it. Inhaling the smoke, while tasting it and letting it out with all the worries and regrets. I know cigarettes are injurious to health, but it's my only companion available with me.

Just when I was about to inhale the next smoke, Jiya popped in the restaurant. While seeing me smoke she just made the most disgusting expression along with coughing. Looking at her no sooner I had to crush the cigarette.

"Err…what a waste" she responded. I did not bother to response and picked one of the boxes and started placing them at its proper place. Jiya arrived near the box and showed her concern to me by helping me to lift the box.

"Ooo…I guess the restaurant turned out to be a battle ground" she stated – "Who said so?" I responded in defense.

"See the red paint everywhere. It's of no sense to lie. Your facial expression depicts everything." Jiya expressed.

I just adjusted myself on one of the chairs and felt as if my heart is sinking. For a while I did speak and just looked outside the window where there was silence spread allover.

The backside of the restaurant was totally opposite. Long green grass – fluffy green grass – waving and rustling in the breeze – interspersed with weeds and meadow flowers – spread along – attached with a small lake – birds chirping while frogs jumping – it was perfectly god's creation.

Silence breaks when Jiya speaks, "At least share, it's a good exercise. Might be I can help you." Quickly I explained the whole scene to her. All I wanted was some idea to get Tasha back to life – back to me.

"Dude, you are an idiot, you're goona regret it if you interfere in her life like that. Even if you want to change her change her slowly and gradually. It's been past six years and some months she is living with her old memories only." She stated.

I kept my eyes fixed on the view and scoffed, "Now what can I do? Please suggest"

Another moment of silence passed, and the next second Jiya smacked me right across the head. "Oi! What are you up too? Why are assaulting me? What was this for? I winced as I rubbed the back of my head.

"I'm trying to check do you have something stored in it or it's an empty head, idiot.

God, I thought boys know all the tricks to please a girl. But he proved me wrong." Jiya responded with a playful smirk.

"Let me give the famous rules to please a girl" she winked while removing the wrapper of her kitkat to eat.

1 – **SMILE** (even if she ignores)
2 – **TALK** (even if she does not response)

After the first two rules she cracked the kitkat with her teeth and further went on with the third fourth rules.

3 – **RESPECT** (treat her like a princess)
4 – **PLAY** (play tricks to make her laugh)

"Ummm...she responded while licking the chocolate that where stick on her fingers.

5 – **GRAB** (if she leaves)
6 – **COMPLIMENT** (even when she looks ugly)
"But she never looks ugly" I shouted out. On which I received a death glare from Jiya. I smiled shyly and said, "Please continue."

After every two rules one bite was necessary, "these chocolates are delicious I must say" she painted in her soft voice.

7 – **CONVINCE** (when she is in doubt)
8 – **PROTECT** (to make her feel secure)
9 – **JEALOUS** (make use of it)

"That all" she flinched. I frowned but nevertheless, didn't argue.

"And the last" she winked with a proud smirk while carrying her bag on her shoulder walking towards the exit with her delicious chocolate in her hand.

My eyes widened in surprise, "What was the last rule?" it made me feel as Tasha happiness was one of the most important possessions of my life. Slowly she started making sense into my silly world.

"Oh c'mon. Please tell" I pleaded while running behind her.

"Grab your breath, if you follow all the above rules. Than I'm sure the tenth rule automatically you will come to know. As boys are damm good at it" she spurted out with a smirk and left while taking the last bite.

"**It's Kiss.**" She smirked.

And she left; I just raised an eyebrow and looked at her cynically. I tell you, I don't understand why these girls like to keep secrets.

Ehh…did not offer even once her kitkat. Wow…she helped in the most amazing way which one can't even define – and at the end the last rule is suspense.

No wait…I guess she said its kiss…Ayan you have lost it. Welcome to the insane world. You are going insane. Ehhhh….KISS….FORGET IT.

I must say these both sisters are highly opposites. One, doesn't needs anyone's help the other is willing to help. Tasha stopped living her life while Jiya lives to the fullest. Ehhh…both are extreme case.

It was decided by me, that at home I will not to talk to her. Will talk only at work place, or else God knows when she will get angry again.

Rules Needs To Be Put Into Action

(The first three rules implemented)

The following day we did not talk more. Just continuing our regular work. There was a silence between us, followed by confusion on my face while Ayan just did not pay attention at all.

Before I could avert my gaze, Ayan's eyes found their way to mine and our gaze met. Instead of pulling my eyes away in an embarrassed style, simply glared at him, in which he replied with a sweet pleasant **Smile**.

Shaking my head, I took my eyes off of him and focused on what work was left to be completed. My eyes got struck towards the container of water, opening the container that I packed for myself, I brought it up to my mouth to quench my thirst and as I swallowed, I quickly looked in Ayan's direction again.

On my surprise I found, Ayan strolling towards me, carry a smile plastered on his face. Though I ignored his smile gesture, he still kept on showing his concern. Oh crap he's just staring over me again and again.

My heart started thumping fast than normal. My eyes growing wider and making me nervous. I muttered to myself, "Shit" moving some of my hair in front of my face. During that moment because of nervousness I swallowed the whole ocean of water with a great speed.

Within a couple of seconds, I could sense that Ayan came beside me and was standing close to me; I turned my back towards him, I didn't had the courage to face him after yesterday's incident nor I wanted him to know, "how lonely I was". I know; it's weird. What's wrong with me today? Oh wait…I guess I'm just getting too much possessive over my loneliness or might be actually overreacting.

"Tasha" he whined in a high-pitch. By hearing my name from his mouth shiver started entering my body and my eyes automatically shut down due to fear. I spoke to myself that, "Tasha you need to be bold to face him. Be courageous and don't let him view your emptiness." While opening my eyes and turning towards him I made a brave attempt to face him.

His hands were enclosed in front pockets of his jeans having a great pair of jeans fitted with a white t-shirt hugged his chest adding on to his personality.

Ok quick Tasha think of something else…quick quick quick…Right, but what?

He mumbled, "Hello, Tasha".

I made all the possible efforts to ignore him, and pretended to continue my work further. Sensing my ignorance, Ayan mumbled, "Tasha I need to ***Talk*** to you".

I did not respond and started to walk forward and continue my work, but I never made two steps away within a couple of seconds he grabbed my arm with his arms and applying a tremendous strength turned my body around and made me face towards him while dragging me towards him. The distance between us was lessened. While I was dragged towards him, my eyes were closed because of fear.

Of course this becomes increasingly worse when you ignore someone. Why do I suddenly get the feeling that I'm in a police station getting caught up in trouble.

My fear was visible, my breathe ran quicker than light. He muttered carrying all the ***Respect***, "Tasha I'm sorry for yesterday".

I slowly opened my eyes and tried to face him again. While biting my lip I glared at him and replied, "Well, leave me" all I could utter but felt as if the police officer released form the cell because he could not prove me guilty.

Looking at my tensed face, he placed his hand behind my waist and drew me towards him more. The distance between us was now almost vanished. My eyes widened, face had a complete blank expression. Before I was about to say, he placed his index finger on my lips preventing me to speak.

"I just want you to smile, life is worth living Tasha. Forget your pain, open your self towards the new the brighter side of life. Give your life one more chance. It's all about taking risks and doing what your heart wants." These were the lines which busted out form Ayan's heart.

Followed by the following line, which completely shocked me and distracted my attention towards him, made my tears fell down. Reminding me of the past and the happy moments which I and Samir had spend together.

"Wherever Samir, may be he always wanted you to be happy". My tears that were streaming down my face did not stop. I could feel a tear from Ayan's eye fell onto my shoulder. Some where even he was hurt by Samir's absence.

Right now, I was nothing but a mute. So I nodded. A moment of silence filled with full of awkwardness.

I tried to pull myself away from him; he kept me at arm's length. He placed a strand of my hair behind my ear and tried to rub my tears. I turned my head towards the other side, disallowing his fingers to touch my face.

I uttered in a choked voice, "You really don't need to be so kind to me". Tears streamed down my face; before I could give further explanation he pulled me towards him wrapping his arms around me with comfort.

I leaned my head into his chest and accepted his comfort while securing my arms around his neck. Tears even rolled down his cheeks.

It was times like this, when I needed some one badly. To console me, to make me understand and to be with me.

After staying in each other's arms for a couple of minutes, we separated slowly, sniffing away the tears and wiping our faces.

I was about to leave, within the mean time Ayan mumbled, "I know you don't need anyone, but a friend is always must to have".

"Can we be friends, Tasha" Ayan asked.

Without giving a second thought, I abruptly replied, "Yes, we are friends". Giving me a small smile, Ayan nodded. I replied him, with a smirk.

After our little patch up ceremony and speech of thanks we continued with cleaning – rubbing – scrubbing – washing – drying – painting – etc etc etc the restaurant. The area occupied was huge by the restaurant. So it was obvious to give fresh new look to the restaurant was time consuming.

While I was painting one side of the wall my cell phone beep-beep with the music, "You & I in this …mmm… beautiful…world…. Ah…ah…aa…You & I in this beautiful world".

Gosh, I painted in distress – how will I answer the phone – my hands are wet in paint – phone ringing in my back pocket – Errrrrrr….can't take the vibration anymore – nor can I remove it from my back pocket.

Ayan stated, "Can I help you?"

I guess it's again no choice in my life, "Yeah…you can!" I mumbled will rolling my eyes here and there. He slowly removed the phone from my back pocket and put it close to my ears.

"Hello! Kabira?" I cheerfully answered.

Kabir sighed, "Tasha, on a serious note stop calling me that."

I made an evil laugh, "HA HA HA….Never."

"Get lost…do whatever you wish. Well do you wanna watch a movie tonight?" he asked.

I glanced at the clock hanging off the wall, it was quarter to six. Today's work was completed and plus the day was tiring too. A little bit of fun was must. I replied, "Perfect, I could definitely make it."

"Oh wait. Get total four tickets Kabira.

Four? I thought it's only you and me going.

Err...no this time you me Jiya and guest-cum-friend are also coming.

Do as I say my dear Kabira.

Err...yeah sure, will do as you say.

Good boy... cya soon, text me the timing of the show.

Cool...will do the need full.

Bye...cya...Kabira...

Don't call me with that_____."

Before he could finish I hung up the phone. Glanced at Ayan just to see his amused expression and all I could make out was he was just shocked by the sudden invitation.

"What?" I asked.

"What, WHAT? I need to ask that." He groaned.

"Oi, chill...we all are going for movie. That's it. Sorry...I did not take your permission but just thought it been busy day – whole day working – need some relaxation."

"Yeah...that true. Great let's go for the movie" he replied with a naughty smirk.

Soon we closed the restaurant and headed towards home. The show timing was eighty –thirty at night, we stripped our work clothes and were in our casual and comfort clothes. Within an hour before me, Jiya and Ayan were ready for movie. All were waiting for Kabira to arrive so that we all can go together.

Finally the devil arrived on his two wheeler – his most important possession – his life – his bike. Before Kabir could even remove his helmet, Jiya hopped towards his bike and occupied the back seat.

I guess me and Ayan no choice except to bear each other. While introducing both unknown person to each other, we headed towards the cinema hall. Kabira and Jiya left while we both walked towards the near by taxi stand.

"Jiya is in love with Kabira" Ayan whimpered.

I diverted my glaze towards him and replied, "How did you come to know?"

"Can make out" he shrugged.

He looked the other direction and said, "But I guess…?"

"Guess? What? I frowned.

"You just can't see that he is in love with you…Jiya in love with him… you see the

Famous love triangle" he stated just peering deep in my eyes.

"Kabir doesn't like me." I stated. He just couldn't. We've always been best friends. I couldn't imagine my life without him; he's always been there for me. I'm sure he is aware that except Samir I can never love anyone.

"We are not going to the movie" I shouted out.

"What? Are you a mental case? Do you need some doctor? He shouted this time.

Things were so awkward. Especially I never thought about Kabir that way. I hate such awkward situations. Through all those tensed expression I had to find out some solution. Only one idea could pop in was taking the help of the so called monster – so called my new friend.

Till the time I could say the driver to return back, we already arrived at the cinema hall. Jiya from far already noticed us. We stepped out while walking I asked Ayan, "Will you help me to get them closer."

"Why not? These guys will make great pair?" he chuckled.

AYAN'S WORDS

We arrived home after the movie got over. We all settle in our respective rooms I just happen to text Tasha,

If in case you need something from your room just wake me up...
I'm just a call away...
Just please don't scare me at night...
Thank you...little ghost
Gudnite (smiley face; winked smiley; heart smiley)

Relaxing on my bed; impatiently waiting for a reply from her just passing time by playing candy crush on my laptop. A knock places on the door. One knocks...two knocks...three knocks...

Ugh, wait coming. I must say she is a ghost only; merely only ten seconds have passed me sending the message. And she is already disturbing me; I guess she took the message too seriously.

"Whoa...Ooooo...a...what do you need?' I spurt out instantly without even noticing it's not Tasha but it's here mother standing at the door with a jug filled with water in her hand. While she comes out from the opposite room and removes her tongue in teasing manner and moves down towards the kitchen.

"Opps...sorry aunty; I thought it's the little ghost" I responded feeling extremely ashamed on my instant behavior.

"What? Little ghost?" aunty stated in confusion.

"Nothing…never mind I'll handle it" I replied while taking the jug from her hand and placing it near the bed.

Aunty nodded with a puzzled look on her face and all I want to do is runaway before I say something stupid more.

While she entered the room and said in a soft tone, "Ayan Thanks."

"Mention not!" I shout totally in confusion. Well! Here comes out something stupid from my mouth.

Before aunty could further say something else my cell phone beeps; lessening the awkwardness filled in the room. Thank God!!! Cell phones are not only distractions during important discussion but at times savers also.

"Just a moment" I responded while reaching towards the phone. Surprisingly! New message arrived from Tasha flashes on my screen.

Hmm…scared of ghost!!!
Weakness@@@Ayan.com!!!
Everyone needs to be informed!!!
Wish you luck tonight@@@
(devil smiley; devil laugh; devil scary)

I did not reply rather I preferred to look towards aunty. She was conscious about something as could make out her constant rubbing her palms to and fro.

"Yes aunty, you were saying something" I interrupted her thoughts.

"Thank you son, for your help and support to Tasha. After six years she opted to go for a movie tonight" she replied calmly with her filled eyes.

"Aunty I did nothi…" I answered.

"Umm...may be you did nothing. But I have seen her laughing and giggling with you. Might be it did not make difference for you but it definitely made a difference in Tasha's life" she smiles.

"Hmm...I don't know what to speak on this" it's one of the reaction everyone gives when they receive praises for the things they also don't they did it right.

"Relax kid...Tasha and Jiya are brought by single parent. Tasha's dad died when she was quite young. I made all efforts to fulfill their wants. When she made me meet Samir for the first time though initially I did not like him; but gradually I found him right for her. By seeing Tasha happy with him, my all worries flew away. And suddenly, God had other plan" she speaks while sobbing.

At times it's difficult to react at an unexpected situation.

Just could not understand, what to do or what not to do? I made aunty sit on the bed while sat down on the ground near her lap; holding her hand I consoled her, "she's a strong girl...purely a fighter aunty. She's just focused on her restaurant business."

Rubbing the tear drops from her face she nods, "Hope soon she starts focusing on her life too. She starts loving her life too. Please help her, to come out from this grief Ayan."

"Meeee..." I replied in shock.

"Yes...I guess you can help her out" she replies while shaking her head.

"Well...aunty. I can't promise." I lie. "But definitely. I'll try."

Even thought I wanted Tasha to come out of it. God knows why I did not have the courage to promise to aunty?

So I preferred to lie. Though; my whole intention to come here in this town was to make Tasha happy.

Was back to this material world when aunty interrupted, "Don't try it, just do it." She ordered in the same style like her daughters do.

I guess its hereditary problem in this family. Ayan!!! You will have most tough time of yours in this house. Get Ready!!! To enter a new phase of life.

"All the best…" aunty said and left from the room.

Amazing everyone is a queen in this house. Nobody asks the persons choice they directly just give orders.

Well…its time to sleep now…

It's Beach Time - I

I didn't like to visit places where I don't find myself comfortable, whether the distance was few minutes away from my place or few hours out of the state, I always used to make excuses of not attending any social gatherings. Except visiting those places where I and Samir together used to spend quality time with each other.

Of all the places which we visited together, beach was our favorite. Dressed my self in the most cozy clothes by picking a pair of denim shorts along with a loose pink in color with blue lines printed tank top wearing my flat studded with diamonds ballerinas.

After Samir's death I often used to visit the beach carrying a pair of headphones that played soft music into my ears and an album containing our funniest photographs ever clicked.

Before leaving for the beach early morning I decided to make a quick breakfast for the family. I wanted a change for a while from the loneliness that Ayan pointed into me & and basically I was being facing, so I decided to distract my mind and cook for all some delicious breakfast. This was the only reason why I opted for movie yesterday for not showing my emptiness.

I walked over to the fridge to look for the ingredients I needed to make our top favorite munch, oven toasted multi-grain bread lathered with garlic, butter and full of cheese, along with mouth watering & tempted banana walnut muffins with less sugar, a cup of chopped walnuts and a dash of espresso enriched with darkly roasted, powdered coffee beans.

With some of the disturbance I was doing in the kitchen with the utensils mom sleep got disturb and she happen to enter the kitchen. Finding me in the kitchen while rolling her hair round making a bun out of it she glanced at me with smile and asked, "What are you doing?"

"Hey mom." I greeted as I started gathering all the ingredients mixing the banana mash with butter along with sugar and mixing it well with the flour then placing it in the oven to bake. I did not want my mom to notice that I heard Ayan & her conversation last night so pretended as if was busy in cooking.

"Hie sweetie." She replied, before continuing herself with the routine work. She glanced at me for another few seconds giving me a genuine smile back as I saw tiny tears forming in the corner of her eyes. I quickly understood the battle fight going in her mind.

I stopped my work and reached across her where she was standing and placed her hand on my hand giving her assurance that, "Mom, I'm gonna be fine." I replied, squeezing her hand in support as I sent her a smile. "Form top Samir is looking down on me, and always wishing that I should remain happy, he'll always be alive here with me, in my heart."

Mom's hand flipped over beneath mine and gave me a squeeze back. I kissed my mom and greeted, "happy mornings."

I patted on her back "Go get ready and wake up everyone, yummy breakfast is at your service all you beautiful people in my life" I said with full energetic voice.

Mom nodded and I quickly entered the kitchen again to prepare cheese garlic bread carrying the butter, cheese and bread along on the stove before placing them on pan. I watched the butter melting quickly in the pan, roasted the bread up and down applying some garlic while covering whole bread with grated cheese over the top.

Placing all the hot morning breakfast on the table, along with a jar full of orange juice placed beside it. Waiting for everyone to come and join me at the dinning table.

Jiya arrived mumbled looking at me with a doubt, "So, what strange voice popped up in your head that decided to make breakfast for all early this morning?"

I groaned rolling my eyes slightly at her question, "be lucky today that I am serving you hot breakfast this morning." I replied teasingly at which she stuck her tongue out childishly in reply. We all started laughing at her and the atmosphere lightens by our laughter.

As we all were enjoying our brunch, we heard couple of knocks on the front door. Jiya stood up headed through the living area and towards the door, she opened the door. Rolling my eyes, I turned my face towards the door to visualize who was standing at the door. Astonished to see Ayan, I stood up from the chair and walked towards him.

I came face to face with Ayan, who was in black t-shirt with some words printed on it saying "***A lie is just a great story that someone ruined with the truth***" and in white shorts who currently had his hands in his shorts pockets, looking exceptionally cool.

I uttered softly, "A lie is just a great story that someone ruined with the truth, defines your personality" with a grin and my eyes rotating upside downside teasingly as I said it to my self. Unfortunately Ayan heard it, moving his eyes downside still standing at the doorsteps and once again knocking the door he said calmly, "if a lie can bring a smile on someone's face, it is worth to lie."

"What, there's no need to knock again, just come in don't you understand?" I asked, while raising my one eyebrow holding the door open as I blocked the entrance disallowing him into my house.

Ayan by making some frowns on his forehead mumbled with a grin, "If you will unblock the entrance than only I can step in."

Rolling my eyes I turned behind and headed towards the dinning table, allowing Ayan to let him in the house. Mom seeing Ayan greeted him, "Hello son, where did you go early morning?"

Ayan said with a teasing tone, "Yes aunty, thought to take sign of Uncle on the some restaurant bank agreement papers, along with the other thought to visit this city – as Tasha will never be a tourist guide – so I helped myself."

Everyone laughed at his wit, which I found it absurd. Mom laughing stated, "Sure son, you are welcome for the breakfast." I peered at mom while folding my hands across my chest with lots of irritation and with a number of frowning lines on my head.

"Yes Aunty, first I'll join my self in the yummy breakfast with banana walnut muffins, multi grain hot cheese garlic bread along with a glass full of orange juice to quench my thirst and then continue with the work." While strolling in the dine area, gesturing a big smile on his face he stated adjusting himself on one of the chairs of the dinning table.

Mom stated happily, "What would you like to eat first." I interrupted in between saying in a teasing gesture, "Give him all he'll complete it all in single bite only."

"Well at least take a seat Tasha and wait for me, while I'll take all the single bite." Ayan shook his head as his smile grew slightly, gesturing or either demanding me to sit next to him.

As I adjusted my self next to him, it was the fact that I sat down just a little too close to him, invading bubbles slightly into me. As I continued to eat, ignoring Ayan next to me, my mom and Jiya kept shooting little glances between the two of us. It looked as if the dinning table is the tennis court, where the two players i.e. me and Ayan playing a match and mom and Jiya are the audience enjoying our verbal game. I secretly sent a warning look as I stared to bite into my banana walnut muffins.

"Well, I guess I'll be going." I stated to my mom, having already finished my breakfast. Getting up from my seat, I walked around the table to put my dish in the sink and cleaning the mess.

In the meantime Ayan licking his lips with his tongue said, "Umm… the muffins are lip-smacking" while swallowing them into his mouth. I turned towards him watching him licking the muffins from the kitchen that made a small smile bloomed on my face.

Mom mentioned to Ayan the expectedly breaking news, "that this morning's delicious breakfast is made by Tasha."

On which hearing this news, Ayan who was lip-smacking the cake stopped doing that. Made a quick look towards me by raising his one eyebrow with showing a question mark on his face and shrugged his shoulders. As pretending that he doubts on my cooking skills.

My anger was at its peak, crossed my arms leaned at the door of the kitchen with squint eyes, I said loudly "Shut up."

By hearing my loud voice, Ayan gulped instantly the final piece of the muffin into his mouth as if I would have stolen that final piece of muffin from his mouth. Making a teasing smirk on his face he stated, "Next when are you inviting me Tasha, for dinner specially served and cooked from your hand."

Without even taking a second of time, I rushed towards him and angrily answered, "Never... and how can I invite you; you are already here only..."

"Oh, come on Tasha" Ayan said teasingly, throwing an arm around my shoulder, "You remember we are now friends."

Rolling my eyes, I sent a well aimed elbow hit to his stomach which meant that soon he should drop his arm off from my shoulder and catch hold his aching stomach. "Anyways mom, I'm leaving for the beach, see you in sometime. Love you." I said pushing Ayan on the other side of the wall.

"Leaving, where are you going?" Ayan started his question round again.

I did not pay much attention on his question and started picking up my bag from the floor and collecting my belonging including the headphones, photo albums etc and placing them into in afterwards adjusting the strap to the shoulder.

Repeatedly Ayan kept on asking the same question, to which I finally replied irritatingly, "Going to the beach for a walk, would you like to join me." To which an unsurprisingly answer I received, "Yes, of course. Let's walk."

It's Beach Time - 99

(Using the next three rules)

No sooner we reached the beach. Ayan was excited to visit the beach for the first time as he was new in the city. His excitement was visible in his glittering eyes making it sparkle off and on.

Ayan stated in an exciting voice, "I have been always heard about this beach a number of times. Today visiting this beach will be my pride" completing the sentence with a board smile.

After hearing that line my eyes grew larger, making me astonish on his sentence "What, you have heard about this beach? How come? I replied in a confused tone with a complete blank expression on my face.

Entering the beach Ayan stated "This beach has its own beauty."

While I was removing my photo album from my bag, "Beauty" as in I stated again in complete confused expression. Making me forget about the previous question, that I supposed to ask him.

"Yes my love, the beauty." He answered in his most comfortable style expanding his hands high up in the air, taking a deep gulp of air in and out.

Making an angry face I replied holding the album book in my hand, "Stop being flirt and answer my question."

Looking at my angry face, he raised his both hands and cupped my cheeks allowing my anger to cool down he answered, "Look Tasha down here, the sand beneath our feet glittering brightly in the sunlight. Making them sparkle like a thousand tiny jewels. The open sky up here, appearing so blue and gay. Wish to embrace it in my arms."

I was just stunned by the words; my eyes were widen refusing my eyelashes to shut down by hearing those mesmerizing words.

Adding on more words to the beauty of the beach, Ayan continued expressing his happiness towards the beach, "The waves crashing against the shore. Form distance waves look like white horses rushing towards the shore."

"Hold my hand Tasha; let's have a walk down in the water." Ayan stated while holding my hand, dragging me in the water. Within no time I and Ayan entered in water where the chilled waves tickled our feet's making us dance in it.

"Ayan stop." I claimed pulling my self away from the water while Ayan still applying his force and pushing me in the water. I could see his naughtiness in his eyes as he started splashing the sea water all over me making me wet.

He started with his *Play* full tricks.

"No No Ayan, please don't do that." I stated adjusting my bag's strap on my shoulder and holding the album book tightly disallowing it to drop in the water as I was scared that the book might float with the heavy waves of the sea and still pulling my self away from him but my force could not apply as his grip on my hand tightens every time.

Ayan continued his naughtiness by constantly splashing water all over. I tried a couple of times to run away but always he would hold me tight. Continuous splashing of water on me did not let me have a clear vision as water was coming all over my face. As I was not able to see in on time I lost the grip on the album and the album fell off from my hands in to the sea water.

I screamed with anger, "Wait. My book is sinking in water." Ayan stopped his naughtiness and was in a shock mode while seeing the album floating with the waves in the middle of the sea.

While I regained my vision, from the salty water that was splashing on all over me. I could only see the single view that my album was floating very far from my reach. Felt as if god once again stole my life form me. My life was going far from me, very far from me and I being helpless could not stop it from going.

Again felt the same emptiness when Samir left me all alone to struggle in this cruel world. No doubt every minute Samir's death was hurting me but I could survive with the facts that he left countless number of memories with me. God today washed away all those beautiful memories also.

I cannot express how much I loved him. But used to console myself saying that everybody's time comes to an end, and his was just a little sooner than expected. Even with the burden of emptiness in my life. I still knew that I had innumerable memories that were the only strength that could let me stay alive.

Numbness ran all through my body. Tears were the only thing which was free flowing all the time in me. With full of anger flowing in my eyes I gave a quick look to Ayan. I did not understand what words I should use for Ayan's stupidity. All I could do was to stare at him with an amused expression on my face.

I could visualize a guilt feeling started to build in the pit of his stomach hopefully as he could have helped me but feeling somewhat saddened and at his fault. If he would have not dragged me in water and rather did not splashed water all over me this whole incident would not have taken place at all.

Thousands of questions floating around the inside of my skull, my eyes started to shut and tears started appearing on my face.

"Oops." Ayan stated guiltily, showing somewhat with a childish smile.

I stared at him, still unable to utter a word from my mouth. I diverted my gaze towards the sea and noticed after few couple of minutes the sea appeared to be exceptionally calm. My album was lost in the sea. After gulping my album it seemed the sea was satisfied with no noise in it at all.

Ayan claimed in a low voice, "Did you understand?" I looked at him clueless and replied, "Understand as in what?"

Ayan explained me this time in a firm voice, **"Shades of the sea change, likewise colors of life even change - Sometimes life appears to be blissful as a blooming flower sometime it appears to as stiff as a rock - But what remains constant is the change."**

Hearing this I was completely at a standstill. No emotions where flowing through me. Could only feel the silent breeze which was coming towards me from within the sea. It was only till that time I could recollect my sense when the silent waves' coming slowly to and fro touching our feet's at the shore.

Ayan continued, "Tasha, even god wants you to accept this change. That is the only reason your album float along with the waves. Leave your memories behind and look forward at the different shades of life."

After those conversations, we were both quite for a little while. There was peaceful silence all over breathing the in and out the sea air. Ayan kept on running one of his hands through his hair in a stressed manner.

My bare foot was swirling slowly on the surface of the water, there were barely any people roaming on the beach, plus calmness of the water and slight breeze is prefect to have word with my inner self.

Even Ayan was quite. No words no swords for defense, only silence was spread over all.

My inner self kept the battle on in me. Somewhere Ayan's theory was correct. I answered my self every one in my family even wants me to leave the past behind and head forward towards the future.

"I'm sorry for getting mad at you for something that wasn't even you fault, I'm sorry for trying to wash all your memories in water. With all those idiotic words I have spoken all along the conversation it's oblivious to say that I'm probably the worst friend you've ever met." Ayan justifying, all his emotions with pain.

I shrugged my shoulders a bit but could not control the small smile which was forming on my face. "Hey, it's fine." I said while placing one of my hands on his arm soothingly.

We were still walking at the edge of the water where in short times intervals the waves used to come over our feet making them splash over our feet and go. However, we had actually been keeping a less- serious conversation for the past half an hour or so.

"Let's play a game" Ayan exclaimed by breaking the silence completely. I asked, "Play what?" with full of butterflies of curiosity coming in my mind.

"Is he crazy or somewhat like that? With a question mark in brain", I stated to myself with disbelief while adjusting the strap of my bag properly to my shoulder.

"Umm… you are thinking right", Ayan mumbled with carrying some sort of wickedness in his voice. "What? I did not say anything loud about your madness", I said in full of astonishment and started fiddling with my hands.

"Oh! That means you think I am crazy" Ayan said in a firm voice while making a smirk on his faces and some countable numbers of frown on his head.

"Oops…No, no I did not mean that way", I interrupted abruptly to give an explanation to him with carrying a childish smile on my lips wondering, why I myself only said about his craziness.

"What game shall we play?" I instantly quoted so that the topic gets changed and Ayan and I do not land up into long argument. After hearing this Ayan grinned followed with a big smile.

"So we shall play, what's there stored in your heart" Ayan claimed in an amused voice while moving his fingers in a magical way in front of my eyes, as if he thought I would get interested in playing the game.

After his explanation finished, I looked up at the sky, asking to God, "What is he made up off? How childish he is, he wants to play the rapid fire game. Answer wants strikes in your head first", I muttered to myself keeping a safe distance to him so that he is not able to hear it.

When I glanced over at Ayan with dry eyes, I saw that he was all set ready in his mind to play the game with me. So I shrugged my shoulders in front of him with not at all high level of excitement to play, I utter "Bring on the game."

"No wait, he said in a loud voice. Adjusting himself at an empty space on the beach he occupied his place and sat down which was near the shoreline. So that we could have a clear view of the shades of the sea while, continuing with our game.

"Come Tasha, make yourself flexible and sit down. After that we shall start with our game" he said.

I reached towards him, adjusted myself next to him, "start with your questions?" I said in an irritating tone.

"As you say so... Princess" Ayan stated.

"Hmm...start" I commented turning my face slightly from Ayan to the sea.

Before starting the game Ayan had raised an eyebrow in question stating, "Tasha, you really need to be fast, frank and carrying a valid reason for your answer."

"Reason" I stated with a small stare towards him which lasted only a couple of seconds before I cracked a small smile and chuckled slightly.

I said, "Cool...now shall we start the game."

"Towards you the very first word, answer quickly with reason." Ayan said.

"Sky?" Ayan stated.

"Birds", I claimed. "And why?" Ayan followed with my word.

"Because they are free to fly. No border can stop them to fly", I quoted with a smile.

"Hmm", Ayan smiled.

Next word he stated, "School?"

"Old memories – best days of life" I said.

"Life?" he claimed.

"Struggle – because god tests those whom he really loves" I quoted carrying a dry smile on my face.

"Sea?" he further asked.

"Waves – it never gets separated from the shores, and even if they get separate they come back." I said with loading my eyes with full of tears but disallowing myself to cry. Ayan just looked at me with a blank expression.

Taking a pause for a second he further stated, "Friendship?"

"You – helped me to strengthen my soul" I quoted in a soft but in a teasing tone, while diverting my gaze from him towards setting my sights on the beautifully calm waters that lay in front of us.

While I diverted my gaze back to him from the waters, still could make out that Ayan was stunned by receiving that answer from me as he was yet holding that blank expression on his face.

Getting back in his senses, he rubbed his hair gently and said, "Night?"

"Stars — have the authority to shine in darkness" I claimed. Ayan again captured a smile on his face.

"Love?" Ayan said in low tone.

"Love...Hmm...is U Me & Fate" I commented in a sad tone while bring my knees up to my chest as I also brought my arms around to hug them tightly.

Sadly, all this resulted from my little outbreak; Ayan sending me the most annoyed and impatient look. I understood his confusion so before he could say I interrupted and explained, ***"U = a boy + Me = a girl + Fate = binds & breaks*** them. Running my hands through my hair impatiently, I continued, "Let's leave now. It is getting late."

Before Ayan could respond I lifted myself up and started walking towards the exit of the beach. Following my steps Ayan even started walking towards the exit.

Before we could exit from the beach, his hand entangles with mine and he pulls me to close to him. He ***Grabs*** me into his arms with passion. His body again sends currents to my body due to his close proximity. By his sudden behavior, I was in an astonish state and just blankly gazed in his mesmerizing eyes to get my answer of his sudden behavior.

"You are just beautiful — in you own way" he ***compliments.***

His lips touched lightly against my forehead, as if giving me an assurance I'll be always be there for you. After the gentle kiss on my forehead he let loose my hand and started to walk, leaving me there stand alone on the sand with a blush on my complete blank face.

His gestures made me smile…. which was worth the while….

Before I could demand an explanation, he frequently quoted "let's arrange a secret date for Jiya and Kabira!!"

Surprised at this line, "Except me, no one calls him Kabira." I stated with anger. It's stupid how his words remind me of both an Angel and Devil sometimes.

"Don't be silly, did you really think a date is a right option?" I commented with confusion. "No offence honey, but please don't use your little brain" he smirked after saying sooo… I ignored his comment.

"So what's goona happen?" I asked him as I followed his footsteps.

"Nothing…just do as I say. Next week we have inauguration of our restaurant so before that we will arrange a lake side view dinner for both of them; provided you help me and don't get angry."

"Angry… Ahhh…hurry…we are getting late. Let me know how can I help you?" I responded. Till the time painting and furniture work will get over.

A Day Before Inauguration

And a million thoughts were running through my mind. One, everything should work according to the plan…And two, tomorrow is a new beginning….

Please God, please be with me through out.

Tired of working, I occupied a space on the kitchen counter while just peering at Ayan for his continuous efforts one, in bring up the restaurant business and two arranging a date for the two idiots.

A theme park rides starting churning in my stomach reminding me that I haven't eaten anything since morning. My search engine starts all over the kitchen to find something to eat. My eyes rolling over & over but not matching my taste.

I jumped down from the counter when my eyes light up seeing the supreme cheese bust

pizza in the hands of the monster. Ewwh…its melting cheese… Oh God!! I can't resist it.

"Are you hungry?" the monster speaks…

"NO…are you kidding? I shrugged. God knows why the hell I denied.

"Ha ha ha…don't tell me Tasha you also do dieting like other girls??? Anyways your size always reminds me of a toothpick." He chuckles. "Come and join. You are working since early morning and I'm sure you are hungry too" he adds.

"Umm…Coming… I searched through the cabinets and fridge to see what I can find. I pulled out two bottles of coke from the fridge and hand one to Ayan before taking my place back on the counter next to him.

Just as we took one bite of the melting cheese pizza, Jiya walks in through the door and straight in the kitchen. "Nice aroma…" she mumbled while taking the pizza in her hand and like a hungry tiger starts eating. I don't know exactly but there is something definitely different about her.

"You cut your hair." Ayan unexpectedly response. While I was just trying to figure out and he was fast than me.

"Yeah!!! Just thought for a new look." Jiya answered while waving her hair in the air.

"So what's the occasion?" I interrupted.

"Nothing… Jiya spoke but Ayan joined in the line, "Nothing! Just today Jiya will say those three magical words to Kabir.

"What??? What?? What?" we both commented with total astonishment? The coke which I was drinking spits out from my mouth by the sudden dilemma.

"OMG…No I can't do this?" Jiya mutters while going to and fro because of nervousness.

Ayan jumps down. Blocking her way while holding her from the shoulders and stated, "Relax… if not today than it's never. Express your feeling. If he stays than he was always yours, and if he leaves then understand he was never yours."

His words had the power to fall for…my heart pumped faster than normal.

"But I can't say it" Jiya nodded. Ayan exclaimed, "You can; you will."

She nods in a negative way while Ayan just smiles and blinks his eyes.

"What if…what if he rejects?" Jiya fumble in her words.

Ayan took a deep breathe, "C'mon honey, no boy is mad to reject a girl like you."

True, I said to myself. No one can is stupid to say a no to a girl like Jiya. She is a perfect combo of beauty and brain. Oi… wait. What did he say? Did I actually hear that? Honey???

I officially started to worry. God! I wanted to kill him. Is this, what people call it? – *Jeloussssssssssssss.*

"Alright, I'll try." She shrugged while rubbing her hair with a bit of worry and she left.

While Ayan shouted, "Be on time."

My brains were giving no command to my body, making me freeze at that moment. My eyes widened, mouth slightly open due to shock while confusion running everywhere in the air.

"Hello Princess, are you alright? While shaking me he grinned.

"Ooo…now princess some times honey" I muttered to myself. Before he could say further I barge in and stated rudely, "Do you feel Jiya can say it? Is it the right way? Will Kabir say yes? What if he says no? Will my little sister take the rejection? Thousands and millions of thoughts playing Olympics in my head.

"You too relaxxxx…you sisters are so alike. She will say it without giving a single thought. Just work fast and Trust me." He responded.

"Where you can't say it, chocolates can say it!" he commented with a smirk.

"What? What did you say?" I reacted totally confused.

"Nothing Princess, don't use your brain. Anyways you don't have it." He stated.

"Ehhh…Err..." I groaned but did not bother to speak further.

Food was ready – tables were decorated– flowers were set – candles were glowing – aroma was pleasant – balloons were everywhere – waiters well dressed – music playing soft – made them all perfect.

The whole restaurant was ready for its new innings.

------------------------* * * * * * *------------------------

Removing my phone form the pocket – abruptly dialing their number – waiting for their reply – times beating faster -

They were the first two guest of our restaurant who were called a day before the inauguration. It took lot of hard work to invite Kabira. I must say answering his hundred of question is not an easy task. Ever lie needs to be justified.

My phone beeped: new message arrived!

On the way – heart smiley heart smiley

Jiya.

"Seems someone is blushing in the messages" I winked moving my direction towards Ayan. On my surprise I found him biting his nails from his mouth; almost all nails must have achieved the sharp edge.

"Oye…wow…ho… someone here is nervous too" I smirked while placing my phone in my back pocket.

"Nervous…No…Not…Never" he shrugged hiding his emotions.

"Typical boy…will never show his true emotions" I winked with a playful smirk.

He showed the most disgusting expression he could ever make. Till that time Kabir happen to enter. The man in black shirt– well built – perfectly dressed for the dinner – and must not forget his perfect dimple adds more to his personality.

Waiting anxiously for Jiya; Kabir smirk "Oolways late!" while tossing his cell phone up and down and Ayan constantly gazing his eyes on the watch. I myself was enjoying being an observer.

Jiya enter with backless white sequence dress – black stone studded necklace- perfect black stilettos – amazing smoky eye shadow – hair tied in French knot with some hair strands coming out – and last but not the least pinky lips wearing a killer smile plus she knows all the tricks to attract boys; before coming close to us she stops lifts a little bit of her left leg showing her toned shinning leg while pretending to adjust the strap of her stilettos.

Uhh…Hottieee…Sexy….I'm sure the boys must be clean bowled….

On seeing her Kabira spontaneously spurt out, "Beautiful" without even once blinking his eyes. He was constantly staring….really constantly staring….So was the case with Ayan too. But don't forget he is too smart.

He walked forward towards her, hugs her gently and places a soft tender kiss on her cheek and stated, "You look gorgeous tonight."

I tried not to be too affected by Ayan's gesture.

Well, I tried…. (It was a mixture of emotion of confusion and anger…but eeee…Anyways neglect it…….its actually jealous)

While at this action I gazed at Kabir, he looked furious with confusion. So some reaction is must. He too walked towards her I guess to kiss her but she flips sideways and walks towards me; making him more angry.

"That was rude Jiya" I stated softly in her ears while hugging her.

"JEALOUSY is a part of love my dear sister; and at times it works too. Chill…tonight I'll tell him what I feel about him. Ooh!! Lord…please be with me me me me" she responded.

"Calm down Jiya. Just breathe." I winked.

Ayan interrupted and said, "Your table is set near the lake."

A moment of silence passed by…if I know Kabir he was puzzled – and Jiya got tensed – well only I left than I was also confused.

5

4

3

2

1

Ayan speaks, "me and Tasha need to complete the rest of the work of the restaurants. So I guess we need to leave now only."

Kabir ran a finger through his silky hair, "What work left out? Can we help you too?"

I looked up at Ayan he was confused to answer so I took over the case, "Hey Kabira, we need to list out the invitees for tomorrow's opening plus we need to bring out gifts for the entire guests. So in that case we both can't make up tonight with you guys."

"And basically you are here; to taste the food" I lied.

"Well; in that case I'll eat everything. I'm starving" Kabir shakes his head.

Jiya and I looked at each other and just laughed. All boys are impatient when it comes to food. "It's okay, enjoy…We shall leave now" I stated while diverting my gaze towards Ayan to move.

Before Kabir and Jiya made their way towards the lake I shouted out, "Do give me the review of the food?" with a smile on my face.

And here we were about to leave; Ayan calls the waiter and hand over a packet. Whispers something to the waiter but I could not understand. I tried hard to look at the words printed on the packet and an "O-O-O-O" started forming on my face.

I was still perplexed, "I can't believe it".

Ayan's eyebrow furrowed in confusion, "Don't overreact Tasha."

I snapped, "Do you really need to do this?"

"Whoa, chill", Ayan commented while walking forward, "It's necessary, you just keep your mouth shut."

"What? Are you trying to say Liquor chocolates will help her out?" I abruptly stopped while walking behind him.

Before I could scream in the restaurant; and before Kabir and Jiya would come to know. Ayan wrapped up my mouth with his hand and dragged me straight out of the door. Again, I began to sprint in but he gripped my elbow, swinging me straight into his chest with force.

His eyes grabbed my attention.

"If you can't get love in your life; please don't ruin Jiya's life. If I have planned something it is all for a reason. Just don't let your emptiness shadow over Jiya's happiness" he *convinced.*

My breathing was getting out of control, not that his words were harsh – but because I was scared. *Is it I don't want my little sister to be happy? Is it I was that lonely that I cannot see anyone happy? Is it I'm too cruel towards life?*

In those mental fights, I realized that still he had his arms securely wrapped around me. I mentally shook my head and began to pull away.

"Let me go…"

"Why? Yeah…of course! So that you can go somewhere, sit alone and weep like a helpless girl" he words came like swords bruising me all over.

"Well! That's none of your business. Please let me go." Struggling to escape from his grip. His eyes were still intently fixed onto mine.

And he let go.

For half a moment; we forgot the world and just faced each other. Gradually; I turned and started moving from his sight.

I dare you…

I dare you…he comments.

I stopped walking, "Err…dare for what?"

"Lovely lady, I dare you for the liquor chocolate. Take one." His voice had the command to make me shiver.

Stupid

Idiot

Nonsense

All I utter within seconds and walked away.

The Kiss

I woke up with a cramp in my neck. As I awkwardly massaged the spot, I don't remember anything about last night.

Just something I remember was –

1- Jiya arrived late
2- I ate the liquor chocolates
3- I was on terrace
4- Kiss

Rest I remember nothing. Jiya was already awake and dressed too. That means:-

1- She was ready for the breakfast.
2- I'm late.

I glanced at the watch showing nine passed ten minutes. Oh my god! Late…I'm late.

Jiya looks at me carrying the most annoyed look on her face.

Eeeeee…She lets out a cry in frustration. She looks cute when she's annoyed but I must know the hell; why she gave me that look and walked out of the room.

Hope I did nothing wrong last night. Well, forget it… Now I need to get ready and reach the restaurant as it's a very important day - *THE INAGURATION DAY.*

I lazily turned on the hot water and waited as the shower got my desired temperature. The hangover was too hard; I guess I had a lot many chocolates. When I got under the hot water, I began thinking of the restaurant.

To suit the theme of our restaurant and to create the perfect atmosphere, the days dragged on and before I knew it, one whole week was almost over in painting are desired shades.

Our restaurant was situated in the centre of the city. Location plays a vital importance for the success of any restaurant. As it was placed in the heart of the city, the new look of the restaurant will definitely drive people to visit it.

When I got out and grabbed my towel, I looked at myself in the mirror. And continuously thinking; about the restaurant and its desired success.

The next step was preparing the menu. The layout and design is just as important as what's listed on the menu. After all, it's essential as customers keep coming back because they love food. We collected all over the country's best chef. Lined up with the chef's all the details about the food industry. The likes and dislikes, new variations in the food business, new arrivals and latest food trends were all gathered.

All these were stressful days working hard over the launch of our restaurant. But all we were excited because we finally were going to show the amount of hard work we invested on our dreams.

While drying my hair; setting it in a high ponytail. Fitting in a white dress which I selected for this occasion. The thoughts of restaurant flew away when Jiya knocked the door and said, "If you are ready, than shall we leave?"

She was rude.

"Yeah! Just a minute; I'm coming."

I was late, rushing down the staircase – finishing off my orange juice; I'm out the door and heading towards my car.

While Jiya waited for me near the car, since morning carrying the most annoying look. This is going to be one long car ride to restaurant, if she is not going to tell me what's wrong.

"Morning Jiya." I smiled while turning the car on.

She returned the greeting with the most fake smile. I hope everything got well yesterday night with Kabir and her – hope she expressed her feeling – hope he too has the same feeling for her – Err…too many hopes.

As we pulled into the parking spot, Jiya wasted no time getting out. I took this as the perfect opportunity to speak with her quickly about her date.

"So what did Kabir say" I questioned.

She turned and gazed at me, "what he can say; definitely a yes."

"O-oh…wow…that's great news. You are happy, aren't you?" I hugged and asked clearing my throat. "So you finally met your soul mate" I teased in a normal manner.

"Um…Yes" she smiled with shyness.

"Then, what's wrong since morning with you? I questioned again.

She squint her eyes, making angry faces and answered, "Nothing is wrong with me; it's you who went wrong yesterday night?"

"Night?" I gulped.

I leaned over the car and waited Jiya to update me further with yesterday night's scene. Jiya started, "Liquor chocolates! I just kept them on the bed and you ate them all."

Oh my god. I think I just liked the taste. I remember I moaned in pleasure as I greedily ate the second…and the next and the next till I reached the sixth I guess.

"How many did I ate in all?" I asked in confusion.

She gave me a death glare as if I demanded Kabir from her, "You ate six of them including the left over chocolates crumbs in the box."

"My calculation was right" I just said that to myself.

"What are you doing?" Jiya went on further.

You burst out laughing – started laughing so hard – clapping like a retarded.

I rushed near you to seize the packet from your hand containing three more chocolates; in the meantime you ran outside the room and locked me inside the room.

"Than, what happen?" I asked innocently.

"The rest of the adventure, you need to take updates from Ayan" Jiya smirked.

"Ehhhh…Ayan" I thought.

All day work, we decided to organize a small dinner for all our family and friends and to beware about the capabilities and qualities of our staff. I and Ayan made sure, that every important person was invited and there attendance was anticipated. Ayan already arrived at the restaurant early morning, while I and Jiya just entered.

Ayan too gave me the most awkward look; made me tensed about yesterday night encounter with him. Jiya started her conversation with our staffs. While I was just standing and thinking "Ehhh…hope I wasn't stupid last night".

I walked close to him, naturally to know more. He ignored and walked away. "Idiot, Monster" I utter to myself.

"Ayan I need to talk to you?" I whispered walking near him.

"Not now, I have work Princess. I can't be late like you." He answered with rage in his voice.

I know I'm late. But I'm sorry.

"You need to be sorry, for lot many things…Princess." He commented while walking towards the kitchen direction.

It was hard to gulp those words. But for god sake let me know the exact scenario, I remember but I remember very less. I walked behind him towards the kitchen.

"Those liquor chocolates weren't yours!" he growled in frustration.

"Well, they didn't have your name on it!" I giggled.

He groaned in irritation, within a fraction of second I was seized by the waist, he dragged me towards him while lifting me up and making me sit on the kitchen counter and peered deep into my eyes.

It is true; that I was fascinated by his eyes. His brown eyes were full with anger. I gasped due to fear, our eyes just stayed locked. His grip was tight enough to ensure I wouldn't go anywhere.

I saw a flash of amusement in his eyes right when his lips formed into his famous smirk.

"So you want to kiss me?" he was referring to last night encounter. That means the last thing I remember was the kiss, and it was not my dream but actually I thought or I did? Oh god….

I actually didn't know what to say, I was trying to get over from his grip. So I began struggling to get out of his hold and let out a nervous laugh, "I know, as usual you are making fun of me?"

He looked offended. "You know Tasha, it's a good thing I have such high self esteem. That I didn't allow you to kiss me?"

"Ehh…Oye…you mean your self esteem is so high; that you can't kiss me." I groaned in aggression.

"That means! You want me to kiss you?" he winked.

After several more minutes hitting him and more struggling, he whispered leaning into my ears, "Princess, if you don't stop hitting me, I swear I kiss you!

And

You can't handle this."

Half the time, I don't understand should laugh at his smartness or get frustrate on his madness. Whatever, it is I kept on hitting him.

"Can't handle! What do you mean? I groaned in irritation.

"You know Tasha, you can't do this?" he replied with a smirk.

"Why I can't do this?"

"Because you can't – Yeah! You understand what I mean – you need guts for doing this – and you are just lost in our own sad world – kiss needs passion – it's a beautiful feeling – basically you are a coward – so you can't kiss." He stated.

If I don't rush into things, if I don't prove myself, if I don't do things in the moment…if I don't…..if I don't….

I grabbed him by his shirt's collar and pulled him close to me. Without giving a second thought, I titled my head… and my lips crashed against his lips. My lips brushed against his lips making his surprise gesture get relaxed, and Ayan kissed me back.

I could feel his warm body attached to mine.

Realization hits!!!!!!!!!!!!

I quickly pulled away from Ayan, pushed him away from me and walked out of the kitchen. While I walked out of kitchen, I was shocked to see Samir's Mom at the launch of the restaurant.

The worries had disappeared and joy was knocking our door. I was even happier as for the first time after Samir's death; Samir's mom would be also attending the launch of our restaurant. Since after the death, his mom never had any word with the outside world. After his death, I have always seen her staying in bed all day. No communication at all with people. Her feelings her thoughts could not be judged by anyone of us. Her face used to look very pale, dull due to grief. No pleasure she used to feel in any activity of life. Her breathe was moving but her mind stopped at the time where Samir left us.

At times she often used to speak or think of suicide. After hearing all those words some one us used to be with her all the time to encourage her, to boost her energy. The upcoming of the restaurant will definitely raise a hope of ray in her heart this was the only positive feeling which I and Samir's dad were carrying with us.

All I feel is where God cannot come, he definitely sends his angels to rescue their devotees. And for us Ayan also appeared as an angel holding his magic stick in his hand, sprinkling some magic upon us and taking all our woes.

It appeared like a dream. Sooner the restaurant was constructed like the modern era, new shades was painted on the walls, felt as if the walls were communicating to each other. New furniture acquainted all the space in the empty area. The whole restaurant was decorated by flowers and candles to welcome our guests for tonight. Everything was most lively in the restaurant than before.

As this was only possible because of Ayan.

A Business Trip

Returning to home after the launch, I walked through the door of my house that night; I rushed in my room upstairs and stripped myself of my all day work clothes. I decided to wear a pink color pajama with red color cheery drawn on it. With a comfortable blue color t-shirt and covered with a thin cotton jacket.

Taking a quick shower and wearing my decided pair of clothes, I laid down on my bed taking my soft pillow in my hand, folding it and hugging it tight to my chest, I smiled as I thought about the kiss – and it was beautiful and amazing.

The following day Ayan and I had to leave for making the arrangements for the other restaurant which was situated in the hilly regions of our country. As it was a cool highly region so it was also tourist attraction.

Ayan would be ready by sharp by 7.00am. The journey was long so we gathered all our belongings and were ready to leave. I managed to get ready, there was an awkward feeling forming in me after the kiss.

Great, just great.

This entire blunder is created by me

Thanks to me.

I was in a red and black formal dress with the perfect pair of wedges shoes. The red top was bit tight at the top followed by the black skirt giving a slim fit to my body. The wedges were black in color with gold patterns drawn around the shoes.

As Ayan and I were attending the meeting for our other restaurant we both need to presentable.

Soon I got out of the elevator and exited my building; I instantly spotted Ayan leaning against his car.

He was wearing a light blue shirt and black formal pants, his hair was elegantly combed. When he spotted me he stood up straight and eyed me from head to toe.

"Tasha. You look stunning". He complemented, walking with me to the passenger door and opening it for me.

I felt the air if filled with awkwardness.

"Thank you" I spoke as I got inside. Placing my belongings at the back seat of the car.

We almost had to cover a five hour distance so as to reach to our desired destination. The drive was a bit long. The radio was on, could hear melody of the pleasant songs that was playing. I raised my one eye brow and tilted my face towards him and with a smile I spoke, "you have fantastic collection of songs".

He nodded his head in return and answer, "yes I know. Thank you".

I just adjusted myself in my seat so that my elbow was rested against the window side and I tilted my head enough so that I had a great view of the scenery on the other side of the window. Ayan was driving continuously and I got to experience the beauty of nature.

The whole region was surrounded by green hills and snow capped peaks. The spectacular cool hills accompanied by the structures made during the colonial era create an aura. The region was draped in forest of pine, rhododendron and oak, experiences pleasant summer and cold, snowy winters.

As it was January month, the region was draped full with snow. The snow flakes were continuous falling and kissing the earth. The snow were crisp, white and shining felt as if the angels high up in the sky were playing with pillows and the pillows burst out and the cottons in pillow turning themselves into show falling on the houses situated in the region.

In the meantime I opened my purse to remove the container of water to quench my thirst. Suddenly Ayan's eye struck to that blue diary which I was carrying along with me.

"What blue book is this?" he asked, glancing at me only for a couple of seconds before putting his attention back on the paved street in front of us. Because of snowflakes the road was extremely clean and clear, no vehicles, no animals, no noise, no nothing.

Glaring playfully at his side, I rolled my eyes, and smilingly I responded, "It's an unknown diary of an unknown person containing some known poems".

Further I answered, "The poems are so well craved portraying the exact emotions of the poet. The poems are engrossed and crumbled in a magnificent style depicting the deep thoughts of the person".

"Poet, how do you that". He responded in a complete shock expression. Further adding to his words, "the person can be a poetess also".

"No" I replied in bit of astonishment.

"No, I explained him the whole scenario about me and the unknown person. From that day onwards I am trying to search him and return the diary to him." I smiled slightly and rolled my eyes.

"Oh, so you want to return this diary". Ayan said, wiggling his eyebrows as a response, I answered simply rolling my eyes up and down and shrugging my shoulders.

"It doesn't seem to me that any day you wish to return this diary to that unknown person" giving me a smirk he replied.

Releasing a sigh, I shook my head as I answered giggling to his line, "definitely I'll return him" rolling down my eyes towards the diary and waving my hand over it.

"Huh, hope so you return it" he asked by clicking his tongue in a mocking way before responding with curiosity. Having a smirk on his face and some sort of naughtiness in his eyes, his eyes started rotating in all directions.

"Whoa easy Ayan, I'll return it." I offended.

While driving, Ayan interrupted in a soft voice "Tasha, every human in their life passes through stones, it depends on the person whether to step over the stones or walk around them. It depends whether to pick the stones up and carry them along with us or you can do is pick them up and set them down by the side of the road".

I clicked my tongue in a mocking way before responding. "Huh, very true said". My eyes had a different spark and rolling my eyes I commented with a smirk, "Is this line framed by you".

"Well, he said no. I stole those lines from a great writer", he replied mockingly, but I could see that there was some pain in his eyes and he really didn't want any one to know his pain".

By sharing and exchanging our thoughts, the journey seemed to be short. We did not even realize that the township started. Small buildings designed started appearing, the town wasn't that crowded, it had a small market containing fresh fruits, colorful clothes hanging in the mini stores, some traditional accessories and lot more.

Within couple of minutes we reached to our final destination, our appointment was fixed with Mr. David. Ayan had come all prepared for the meeting. As we had heard a lot about Mr. David, he was much disciplined person with high values in his life. Punctuality was the key to success which he used to admire. Work was worship for him.

Mr. David spotted us, and invited us in his cabin. He was tall young man, having whitish complexion and well shaped French braid. He was on his working attire, a black suit with white button up shirt and black pointed polished shoes, the blazer had a shine hugged tightly to his chest.

Ayan and I arrived on time at the meeting. We both had a long conversation with him. Stress was felt by me and Ayan in convincing Mr. David for leasing his land to us. We both were trying our best and working hardest to acquire this plot.

Ayan said, "This leasing agreement is most beneficial for you, Mr. David. Take my words in this agreement you will not end up in loss".

"Hmm, yeah. Let me think over it again", he mumbled.

He started scanning all the papers presented by us. This time he studied deeply all the agreement papers.

In the mean time he interrupted, "Ayan and Tasha, you both are invited today evening to my farm house for a mini business party."

After saying this much, he glared at me and give a smirk to me and within the next minute he started turning the papers in the file, seemed as if he was pretending to read. This gesture of his made me a bit uncomfortable in his cabin.

Without giving a second thought, Ayan excitedly answered, "Yes of course we will come."

"Your presence will be appreciated" glancing at me Mr. David replied vaguely.

Further he replied, "Will go thorough all the papers, then I'll decide and give my verdict on this deal. In the meantime you people are warmly welcomed tonight for the party".

Ayan and Mr. David had a hand shake and greeted each other. The very next moment I and Ayan exited from his cabin and started walking towards the elevator.

As soon as we entered the elevator, Ayan pressed the ground floor button I hastily asked, "Ayan why did you say yes for tonight's party. We are supposed to leave now only."

Ayan for a few seconds just stared at me with an innocent smile. I uttered, "What" in a confused and curios tone.

Till the time we reached seventh floor from twelfth floor in the elevator, Ayan pulled my cheek and replied with a big laughter, "Sweetheart at times we have to attend business meetings and built our tie ups with business class people."

We arrived at the parking lot; Ayan unlocked the car and started the engine.

Occupying our respected seat in the car, I glared at Ayan, making a pity face I grunted out loud, "I'm starving" as Ayan chuckled at me.

Ayan replied, "I take you to amazing place where we will have an incredible lunch together".

My eyes widening slightly towards those words, placing my hands near my tummy and in low voice I said, "Please drive fast, or else I'll die of hunger only".

He had a grin on his face and politely replied, "Ooh! At your service madam. Fasten your seat belt, this car will now run in the air."

I stopped before entering the car. "Tasha, did you realize" I mutter to myself "In the air." I carried that expression when you just realize something.

"CRAP...Why the hell did I wake up the monster." I muttered.

I shut the door of the car and started walking in the opposite direction.

"Hey, where are you going?" he called out.

"I'm not coming with you. As I aware now you will take your revenge. It's better I'll walk."

"And you will walk at the snail's speed." He grunted.

As I walked in the opposite direction he started moving the car in the backward direction along with me along with making continuous sound of the horn.

"Ehh…Leave me alone, Ayan."

"Hmm, even I said the same words when you forcefully kissed me" he growled out.

My eyes widened in shock.

"I wonder Jiya and mom will think, when they find out you kissed." He winked.

The color started draining off from my face, felt completed paralyzed.

Ehh…felt helpless….

"You wouldn't do that." I stated.

"I can, & I will say to all." He shrugged.

"That's ridiculous. No…no that's actually mean of you.

You forced me to kiss; I mean you forced me to prove myself.

I just defended myself; you…you're goona regret it if you say it."

"You wish so, I'll not say if you just in the moment sit in the car" he commented with a smirk.

"He is such a stubborn guy, will do only things which he likes." I just kept these words with me only. Opened the door of the car and adjusted on my seat.

"Don't go too fast…"

He did exactly what he said; the car was actually running in the air. Till the time we arrived at the restaurant my hair were scattered all over my face, my eyes rolling up and down and my heartbeats thumping fast back and forth.

After recollecting my senses I stepped out of the car, pushed the door of the car harshly making a loud noise of door. Rushed towards and stood in front of him. I stared flatly at him.

He pushed me towards the left side, and started walking towards the restaurant. My anger just ran all through my nerves making me feel annoy.

"You are irritating at times" I muttered angrily.

He shouted with a teasing intent, "Tasha are you joining me or shall I make the food my partner, I mean or shall I have the lunch all alone".

I said, "Don't go fast."

"Next time, you don't kiss me."

"Ehhhh…" this kiss comes in between every conversation.

After hearing this, holding my hands up in a surrender position, I smiled slightly," but natural I'll join you as I am dying of hunger". I stated before dropping my hands and walking alongside Ayan.

As we entered, it appeared to me as a bistro which was skilled in an informal restaurant serving wine. Glazing at the menu card, I stammered and spoke to Ayan, "don't you feel it's an expensive restaurant."

This time Ayan widened his eyes and replied, "Consider it as a treat from me, might be tomorrow you won't even like my presence".

This line made my eyes roll all over; I squint my eyes and looked at him completely in a confused state.

My eyes were demanding an explanation, suddenly changing the topic he spoke, "what shall we order for our empty stomach".

Before I could demand for an explanation, his phone rang. He answered the call and moved away from the table so that one could not hear his conversation.

In the meantime I called the waiter, who looked to be in his late forties as he had slightly grey tint to his hair and facial features were slightly worn out, wrinkles appeared on his skin, smiled at us, "Welcome to Green Avenue, what can I get for you Madam?" he asked in his cheerful voice.

Ayan disconnected his call and approached towards the table and sat in the opposite direction, interrupted "I'll have burger with extra onions in it, tomato ketchup and hot French fries with an extra pinch of pepper sprinkled on it and a medium coke", Ayan rattled off, not even taking a glance at the menu card.

The waiter nodded and noted down the order and said, "Okay, and for the lady." He said, nodding in my direction.

Ayan even turned his face from the waiter towards my direction, "your order" he asked.

"Well...Hmm... "I'll go with a large chilled coke with spicy delight pizza with a combination of corns, onions, jalapeno and red paprika as toppings along with the cheese dip" I said in a clear voice.

Our order arrived, the waiter placed the food at their respective position, "Hope you enjoy your meal and have a great day ahead" he said with a smile before leaving from our table.

By seeing the mouth-watering food there was a glitter in my eyes. I removed one piece from the yummy pizza and took a bite and, utter "Hmm… utterly delicious making my tongue go round and round on my lips.

I closed my eyes in and let out a moan of appreciation, forgetting for the time being that Ayan was sitting in front of me, seeing my expression until I heard a chuckle from his mouth.

"What?' I asked softly, taking the other piece of pizza and giving a small bite to it.

Ayan just watched me giving a smirk and shook his head, replied "Nothing dear".

Decided not give me an answer and started concentrating on his huge size burger and took a big bite.

Next few minutes we were sitting silently and enjoying our meal. After completing our serving dish almost and having our desired coke, "Thanks for the lovely lunch." I stated, playing with my hair.

Ayan raised an eyebrow at my sudden outburst. "What for? The lunch? He answered disgustingly.

"Ooh... mention not. If you wish you can pay the bill" further he stated.

Will stating this line I just gazed at Ayan, with completely nil expression and was wondering that I can never understand this person anytime. He tried his level best to bite my head off but it did not work well.

"Well, cut it out" I stated in a disgusting manner.

Ayan cracked a smile at my last remark, and with a nod on his head, he stated "Not an issue, I'll pay it".

Ayan handed over the cash and accepted his change, we both moved towards the car. Yet some more hours were left with us to attend Mr. David's business gathering. So we decided to book different rooms in a motel and rest for sometime.

Facing Fear

*T*onight by 8 we had to reach at Mr. David's business dinner. Making me feel at bit nervous and conscious about not arriving too late or too early, conscious about my attire should not be too formal or too casual for the occasion.

Seeing my confusion on my face, "Tasha" I heard Ayan's call from behind. I turned around to face him, "Yes"? I replied.

I just wanted to tell you Tasha, he had an innocent smile and with a decent voice he **convinced**, "Everything suits you, your magnetic personality attracts everyone. You can charm anyone without even trying. You look beautiful whatever attire you wear"

After saying these words he rolled his eyes down, I don't know somewhere somehow I was blushing deep inside my heart on his words. For that very moment my cheeks turned pink, eyes glittered with sparks making me happy.

My confusion was vanished the very next moment, I replied "Thank you" with a blush.

He left after that. I decide to wear a black & white mid-length dress with red open-toe heels and a red small purse with golden sequence beads drawn on it. My makeup was normal with just blush, mascara with light eye shadow and lightest pink lip-gloss. My hairs were open kept loose with natural curls.

I was almost ready, Ayan knocked my door and stated, "We need to leave Tasha, or else we will get late. We will pack our bags once we return from the dine."

"Let's leave Tasha" he screamed.

"Umm…coming just a minute" I responded in return. Wearing my golden long round earring.

As I locked my room, and headed towards the car, I spotted Ayan leaning against his car. He was wearing a grey suit with a light pinkish shirt and well polished back shoes and hair was set and combed elegantly. When he spotted me walking towards him he stood up straight and eyed me from head to toe, as usual.

"Tasha, you look gorgeous" he praised and tilted his head a bit and placed a kiss on my cheek (exactly the way he kissed Jiya to make Kabir jealous).

"Thank you" I spoke with a blushing smile.

While driving towards the farm house, Ayan explained to me importance of such social events. The purpose of such gathering was for well-known companies to discuss their upcoming projects and the newly launched projects and how their previous launch had been successful.

As we arrived to the farm house where the dinner was arranged, could observe there bombarded flashes from the cameras of media, that time I realized Mr. David was a very famous renounced personality within the state.

We exited the car, stepping out while Ayan was at the entrance handed the keys to one of valets who would park it in a parking lot. In the meantime I was waiting for Ayan to come back so that we both together can enter the lawn where the dinner was arranged during that I spot Mr. David.

His eyes spotted me, excusing all his guests he started walking in my direction. Now he was standing exactly in front of me. I smiled looking at him & greeted "Hello Mr. David".

He placed his hand in my waist, brought his face close to my left cheek and leaned in to kiss me and replied; "Welcome Tasha".

This gesture of Mr. David made be uncomfortable; fire was burning through my eyes I wanted to push him back and show my anger but all I could do was stepping two steps backward, rolled my eyes down and showed a fake smile.

All this Ayan noticed while he was coming near me, I could sense his irritation towards Mr. David, will his eyes widened due to anger. His gaze met mine indicating his rage towards Mr. David. A grin was plastered on his face, indicating me to come near him. I smiled back to him and excused myself from Mr. David.

I arrived near Ayan trying create a decent distant between us. All I wanted to hug him and just feel secure as his absence was making me feel anxious. My eye lashes turned a bit wet due to the fear of loneliness.

Ayan looked deep into my eyes, I'm sure he could feel my insecurity. As soon as I was close enough, Ayan thrusted me into his chest, placing his lips near my ears he whispered, "Relax, I am always with you – ***to protect you.***"

The tear which I was holding in my eyes, ran through my cheeks along with a pleasing smile. That was the very moment when I grabbed him and hugged him tightly.

We both were together talking around with some of big industrialists and discussing their projects and their constructions. We all talked, listened and laughed within the group. I spotted a tall, slim woman with sharp features and long thick hair approached Ayan from behind.

"Ayan!" she exclaimed, hugging him and interrupting our conversation. She was wearing a white gown with a red bow attached at its waist along with her ocean blue eyes surrounded by make up and her straight open hair making her look elegant and attractive.

"Hi" Ayan replied, pulling himself back. Followed by the other sentence, "how are you, met after a long time" he asked.

I was waiting for him to introduce either of us to one another. Somewhere I did not like the woman hugging to Ayan, as I felt I solely should have this right reserved with me.

The woman moved beside Ayan as she eyed me. "Tasha she was my classmate Roma during our learning sessions of hotel management. While, Roma she is my friend Tasha".

"Glad to meet you" I smiled, extending my hand.

"Nice to meet you, too" she shook my hand, later placing one hand behind his neck and the other in his chest as she leaned into whisper something against his ear. It's obviously we all have big or small secrets in life; and certain amount of privacy everyone requires. Her actions indicated that they knew well each other; their friendship seemed to be quite close as she was trying to taking some sort of claim over him.

And even Ayan was quite oblivious accepting all this gestures. While all her touching and whispering; Ayan's eyes meet mine twice in the last ten minutes and I quickly divert my attention away from him to look at anything else.

We kept our conversation for a few minutes until I excused myself, unable to keep watching them. I kept questioning myself, "why I could not see any other woman getting close to Ayan.

Lost in my own thoughts, struggling to find the answer I headed towards the washroom. All I could find out was I was *Jealous* of Roma. Bit angry on Ayan, as he did absolutely nothing to stop her and widened the distance between them. The fact was I could not bear watching any woman coming close to him.

To wash away these thoughts I opened the tap and splashed water on my face a number of times. I raised my head above and looked in the mirror, from the mirror on my surprise I found Mr. David standing behind me.

I turned behind with a shock, some water which I collected in my hand splashed on Mr. David's face and on his suit making him wet.

I uttered in an afraid voice, "you here in ladies washroom". I could sense his power and dominance which he would try to use on me. Could clearly see the lust in his eyes and his little steps towards me had made all his intentions crystal clear.

He said, "Tasha you look very sexy, I could not resist my self coming towards you." He started walking towards me and automatically my steps moving backwards until the point reached where my back portion hit the wall and I could not move further.

I said in a low voice, "I need to leave, Ayan is waiting for me." His eyes widened on hearing this line. Still he continued to walk towards me until the time came when he was close to me.

He placed one of his hands in my hairs and started playing with it and whispered, "I want you" showing his desperation. By hearing this I pushed him away from me. He grabbed me tightly from my waist disallowing me to move and thrusted me into his chest and continued to grin.

Trying to bring his lips close to mine, I pushed him hard. He tightens his grip at my waist and started licking around my neck and slowly entering into my chest. This time I pushed him harder applying all my strength. The push was so hard that his grip on my waist was gone and he reached at the opposite side. In the meantime I managed to rush at the door and quickly ran outside. I pushed my legs enough, racing as fast as I could tolerate, never dare to look back.

Coming outside where the dinner was arranged, I managed to organize my dress properly. I folded my hands across the chest; walked looking down towards the ground feeling as if was ashamed of me.

I was searching for a place where peace was my only companion and I could weep out loudly. Droplets of water crept swiftly and silently down my cheeks making my agony enhance. My heart…my heart was sinking in the deep black ocean of sorrow. My entire mind was occupied by Mr. David's ill intentions.

I tried to keep my mind completely off from everything. Curling into a tight ball of pain, my eyes squeezed and shut and a strong wave of grief hit me. I muttered to myself,

"Damn…Life is so unfair to me." Still the tears racing down my cheeks making difficult for me to breathe.

Ayan tired to call me a number of times. I rejected the incoming call all the times. After numerous calls, my phone chirped, declaring a new text message.

I opened the newly arrived text.

Ayan : Where are you? I am worried.

I was still angry at him for his behavior towards Roma; her wandering closeness towards him and irritated on an ill mannered, or someone who is discourteous, uncivil or you may even say a vulgar person like Mr. David.

I didn't bother for replying to Ayan, just standing alone and weeping continuously.

After few minutes I heard sounds of someone walking furtively. Before I decided to turn around I wiped off my tears which did not stop running down my cheeks. Within few seconds I turned around to figure out the person who was approaching me. Frankly I wasn't that surprise to find out, it was Ayan who was searching me since long.

"What's wrong Tasha? Why are you not answering my call?" Ayan asked in a muzzy voice.

Due to excessive crying, I found hard to breathe.

I did not bother to answer nor did I pay any attention on what he was saying. I did not even have the courage to face Ayan nor could I make him understand what went wrong with me during the past one hour.

As I was not paying attention on him, he dragged my hand towards him, pulled me and forced me to look into his eyes. My eyes were wet, the eye shadow which I applied was almost spread making my face look shabby. Ayan noticed a scratch on my neck made by Mr. David's nails.

I slightly pushed Ayan, started walking in the opposite direction. Ayan repeatedly kept on asking in loud tone, "what went wrong? Why are you crying? And so on and on his questions followed back to back.

One moment came when Ayan hold my hand and stopped me making myself turn towards him and asked in a soft voice," did someone behaved ill-manneredly with you?"

My eyes squeezed and shut down with tears overflowing alongside my cheeks. I tried my best to raise my head and look deep in Ayan eyes and give a smile. But all efforts went in vain.

Ayan whispered in firm voice,

"Beneath the makeup & behind the fake smile, There's some sorrow hidden since a while".

All could say after listening to those lines where, "Ayan can we please drive and go back to home".

I guess Ayan understood and sadly said, "Alright will leave now only."

Before leaving Ayan said, "I'll go and once say Goodbye to Mr. David."

"No please", I said holding his hand as disallowing him to go to Mr. David.

Supposing Ayan understood my discomfort and pain in my eyes which was again flooded with water. Ayan answered softly, "Alright lets leave towards the hotel, after packing our bags we shall leave."

Headed towards one of the valets to ask for the car. After it was retrieved from the parking lot and handed to us, Ayan thanked and tipped the guy before heading for the hotel.

We adjusted ourselves in the car. He kept on asking the same question, "What went wrong." But I just answered one line, "Ayan, today if Samir would be alive my life would be very beautiful."

"Miss you Samir" I said tenderly without letting him hear this line.

As I turned my face towards Ayan, who was paying very close attention to the road, glanced my way for a couple of minutes. I saw that he had an eyebrow raised in shock, his eyes turned red with wet, a tear rolled down from the edge of the eye on the other side of his face by rubbing that single tear he asked," You uttered something?"

In a shock tone I replied, "No... nothing."

Rest the entire journey till the hotel we both sat quietly without facing each other. I kept weeping facing in the opposite direction where he would not come to know & Ayan drove wordlessly the car as if holding some grief in his heart.

All I could make out is the grief was somewhere slowly killing him from within making him suffer each and every moment.

All I know is, I faced fear...so close...very close.

True Emotions Coming Out

After arriving to the hotel, I opened the front door of my room without even paying attention to Ayan.

As I entered my room, throwing the keys, purse and phone on the bed I started gathering all my belongings and placing them into my bags. While gathering my belongings and placing them for few minutes the same flashback I visualized when Mr. David's villain intentions were noticeable.

Right now, I felt as if I could wish to rewind my life and relive all those beautiful memories with Samir. His absence made me weak day by day. The smiling curves on my lips turned into sad lines depicting deep sorrow on my face. Sometimes, I wonder if it was karma hitting me for some sin I did in the past. But than I made my self understand and believed in fate and if we weren't meant to be together then so be it.

While fighting through all those thoughts I lay on the bed, placing one of my hand on my head slowly closed my eyes and prayed to God for helping me come out of the grief.

After half an hour I was woken up with a repetitive knock on my room's door as I did not even realized when I was fast a sleep. I forced myself out of bed, completely annoyed for being woken up.

I wasn't that surprise to expect Ayan as we were about to leave for our hometown. He was about to knock again when I abruptly opened the door. I looked at Ayan with my squeezed eye and then rubbing them so as to widely open it.

"Hmm…come in, I'll just get ready in couple of minutes till that time you may come in and sit and then we shall leave." I said in a sleepy voice. Ayan entered my room with his mini luggage and made him self comfortable.

While entering he asked the same question, "You didn't answer my text or calls, what went wrong Tasha" Ayan reminded.

"Are you seriously asking me this question now, Ayan?" I exclaimed sadly.

Saying "Yes" he paused waiting for my answer when I remained silent and trying to be busy with my work, he spoke again "Answer me please, Tasha."

"Quit the silence, Tasha" he said in an irritating voice. As if my silence was eating him up. He kept on repeatedly asking the same question a number of times.

The number of times he would ask the number of times those scenes would flash in my mind making me feel sad and dishearten. Ayan did not lose hope and kept on asking the same question till the time my anger started boiling through my veins, watering my eyes.

I refused to cry from anger.

Before Ayan could say further I said in a loud voice, "Stop it please".

I pulled a bit from my shoulders one of the sleeves down of my dress and showed the marks hidden inside and said in a sad tone, "Hope now you can understand what went wrong with me & all thanks to Mr. David." Still refusing myself from crying.

His eyes darken with my words. After seeing those marks he stayed stilled, rubbed his face with his hand, avoiding eye contact with me and those marks on my body. I saw that he had a very guilty look plastered upon his face. It was obvious that it was a hard time expressing how helpless he was feeling on seeing those marks.

"Oh god!" he grunted, starting off his explanation by running a stressed face down his regretful face.

He gathered all his courage and walked forward towards me. I was looking down at the ground because of being ashamed of someone's ill- intentions. He was close very close to me. He pulled back up the shelves from my shoulders placing on its proper positions.

His eyes were glassy looking from unshed tears. It seemed as if he had definitely suffered, getting a glimpse of my hurt.

All he could utter was, "Sorry" I heard.

Tears which I forcefully stopped in my eyes poured out instantly. This time I stepped forward closed to him, as the small part of me which had some feelings for him took over me.

Closing the gap of space between our bodies, he embraced me into his arms. He was very well aware that I was having an inner battle with myself. Without waiting for the other second my hands wrapped them around his neck.

The proximity and warmth of his body had sparks igniting all over me. I tried to move away from his warmth by separating myself from his love and affection. For once my gaze met his gaze. The feelings which we concealed in our inner self were clearly visible.

Leaning forward towards me Ayan whispered,

"Sometimes deep in my heart...
I question life...the reason to be so cruel to me?
Sometimes I wonder am I learning a bit too much...
Little pranks, silly jokes, huge laughter seem to be past season...
Night long thoughts, silent tears are all with a reason...
Sometimes want to ask god...why you let this happen?
Sometimes I answer myself thank god it all happened...
You made my life so beautiful...
Why is life such?
Regrets and good memories come along...
Smiles and tears come along...
All I know is we all have a story and it's all planned by him...

Pausing for a while he panted again,

Let's see how he wants to take our story....?
How he has planned the climax of our life...?"

After hearing this I was so affected by him at the moment that the words were blurted out of my mouth before I had the chance to think about his question and what would be the answer. Before I could keep prolonging my judgment, Ayan's lips met mine. Meeting my lips with his lips made my feelings arrived over the edge.

It was magical, the way his lips connected with mine. His tongue tangled with mine as I drape my hands up his chest, wrapping them around his neck. I was not aware we were moving until the back of my knees hit my room's bed and I fell into it while Ayan accompanied my fall.

Now the distance between us seemed more intense and full with lust.

He lowered his head until his lips meet mine again, kissing me tenderly. His pink tongue, flicking between my lips. He licked; the sensation of his touch burned the flames all over. We began to make soft mewling sounds while kissing; his eyes were wide unable to pull back from me and the pleasure and desire was clearly visible. He slid into me making me feel the most pure sensation of my life; touching every nerve of mine.

I could feel every millimeter of his body inside me, his muscular strength and feverishly hot skin enveloping me into him.

I stretched myself & slowly lowering my head on the bed while still I wrapped my hand around his neck, closed my eyes slowly while closing a tear appeared at the edge of my eye with a smile lingering on my lips.

From my room's window the first rays of the sun grace in my room. At the crack of dawn the sun peaks out from behind the mountain. Before my eyes could open up totally I could see the clouds getting separated allowing the sun to pop up announces a beginning of a new happiness coming along the way.

I woke up to a tangle of sheets and limbs. My arm across his stomach, my fingers tangled with his as I rested my head on his chest. His arms were hugging my waist. I peered up at him to find him peacefully sleeping.

Despite everything I've been through, I didn't regret last night. All I was aware was, I was attracted towards him and did not realize when the attraction turned into love. Now when I am aware that I love Ayan all I want is to unlock all my feeling towards him and let him know this deep secret.

I placed light kiss on his neck and tried to get out of bed slowly, not wanting to wake him up, but Ayan's grip on my waist only became stronger, disallowing me to move away from him and indicating that he was awake somewhere in his sleep.

"Ayan, it's morning leave me we need to leave" I said softly in his ears chuckling into it and he responded by a groan. He removed his hand from my waist and shifted his position, laying on his side to face me. I quickly started to get up and avail this opportunity to get go towards the washroom.

I found his shirt from the last night near the bed, lifting it, putting my hands through the sleeves and buttoning it up on my way across the washroom.

I smiled looking at him, as I got up while I threw my feet over the side of the bed and padded my way to the bathroom to get ready. I was anxious rubbing my hands with each trying to calm myself while moving in the bathroom to and fro. Basically I did not have the courage to face after what ever has happened between us. The feeling was pure but at the same time the feeling contained mixed emotions also.

Anger Takes Over

Entered the washroom glanced myself in the mirror, felt as if every nerve in my body is more alive than normally is. The world falls away, ordinary thoughts and worries are left behind. For that very moment all my thoughts cease and I in a state of total bliss and relaxation. I closed my eyes and my mind drift off.

As soon as I closed my eyes, all I could visualize was the odds of last night between me and Ayan. There was a small window in the bathroom allowing a number of rays of light entering in the bathroom with cool breeze touching my body sensationally while making me remember his touch all over my body.

A blush was painting its way onto my cheeks as I peered myself in the mirror that was attached to the wall in my room.

Although I was nervous and anxious, but somewhere I was happy still did not have the courage to face him.

Confusion ran all through my veins. I was a little nervous about how Ayan would react thinking about the last night.

Truly I did not have the courage to face him. Wondering how he would be judging about me and himself. Fighting with my inner self I had to gather all the strength and audacity to face him.

Rubbing my hands with each other, I unlocked the door of bathroom and slowly uplifted my legs towards the bed to face Ayan. My steps were slow and breathe running as fast as athletics' speed still rubbing my hands aggressively with each other.

I approached towards the bed, raising my eyes from the ground I saw Ayan was awake removing his new shirt from the bag, turned him self, his back was facing me lifting his shirt while pulling up his sleeves and buttoning it up.

While he was getting ready he panted softly, "We need to leave, as it's getting too late. You just get ready I'll just complete some work and come."

When I looked into his eyes I saw an unreadable emotion flashing in him, but I did not even have a second to figure out what it mean.

As I heard that, I shook my head, refusing to think about what happened last night. "Umm…sure." I said suspiciously.

I wanted to ask, "Wait, what's wrong?

Where are you going?

But all could say was, "will get ready till the time you arrive.

"Hmm…I'll be waiting for you down near the car." Ayan answered frantically put his hands in his pockets started heading towards the door. In few seconds he slammed the door loudly and was out from the room.

With the loud sound of slamming the door, a current ran through my body capturing all my nerves shutting my eyes tightly due to fear. Some where I felt guilty that Ayan might regret the last night. All I could feel was that I was incapable of reading Ayan mind.

I recollected myself from his thoughts, lifted my lips up in a small smile while discarding his shirt which was embraced by my chest and wearing my own set of clothes. I dressed myself in a high fitted jean with feminine shirt hugged to my chest and a pair of shoes along with it.

Removed the blue diary from my bag placed it in my hand and zipped my bag while heading towards the parking lot. I was planning to tell Jiya, hoping a confidence boost from her would help me or shall I consult my mom about this. Afraid about how mom would react on hearing this. Could visualize her red eyes and her angry face too, her trust on me would be lost all I would again be alone in this cruel world.

Dialed Jiya's cell number and soon disconnected, dialed mom's number and same disconnected. I did not found enough courage to do so. It was all a mental battle, what to do, what not to do. It was mind-consuming and it would soon turn out to end with a headache.

My inner self was consciously biting me, could not understand how things went wrong. Wanted to have a conversation with Ayan, but after visualizing the unreadable emotions in his eyes, a fear of losing him strike my mind often.

I convinced myself that I should be brave enough to talk to him about last night. I should at least have a right to know what he feels. Why is he suddenly avoiding me? Is it is my mistake only?

Somewhere inside my heart I had a strong intuition that he is hiding some thing. Some secret is yet to reveal. The pain which I could always visualize in his eyes, and which he tried to hide in his smile.

Ayan's words

Half an hour, I guess is enough?

I removed the car from the parking lot, unlocked it and drove fast; very fast. Till the time I reached my destination.

My destination – Mr. David's mansion.

During the drive, all the time I could only visualize was Tasha's innocent face, the pain which she went through. Her sad voice depicting her sorrow.

Her glassy eyes held so much emotion, it just consumed me.

Her…Her marks on the shoulders.

My car entered the huge mansion; definitely he is one of the richest men in this town. I ranged the bell and waited outside impatiently for him to open the door. The door was opened and a maid greeted me, she requested me to sit till the time Mr. David arrives.

Within five minutes, Mr. David arrived.

"Hello, Ayan…welcome to my home."

"Hey, thanks." I returned the words.

"Please be seated, I know you are here for the business." He replied.

"Not exactly." I nodded while rubbing my hands with each other.

"So; in that case I'm ready to collide with your business." He smirked.

My eyes widen on his sudden approval.

"But only on one condition" he winked this time.

Patiently, I sat there and was just viewing his villain's intentions.

"And, what's the condition?" I spurted out loud.

"I just want Tasha to near me and…" he said.

Before he could say further, I stood up.

"Well; thank you so much. I'm glad to inform you that I and Tasha are not interested in doing any business with your company."

On hearing this he stood up too in shock.

"You are creating a big mistake by not colliding with us. Our hotel management is the best in this town. You will be in loss if you leave this offer."

"Well...in that case. I'll like to give you some gift for the wonderful offer you to give to us." I smirked closing my fingers tightly and aimed a punch straight on his pretty face.

Dammit. As I punched him on his face my mind just occupied Tasha's poor face, her helplessness towards the situation. There I go again thinking of her.

Focus Ayan, I said to myself.

Before Mr. David could get up, I pulled him up by the collar and punched that Bastard in the jaw, with so much force and intensity of anger that he fell back.

The blood started draining off from his nose.

I managed to stay him grounded and hit him hard repeatedly on his stomach.

"This is for your wrong deed towards Tasha, next time don't even dare to look at her. I promise next I'll not leave you alive." I winced.

"Hope, this lesson is enough for you." I groaned.

I got up and left.

The Truth

(Part – I)

I entered the parking lot, where I found Ayan leaning against the car. Before I could walk close to him and talk to him. He noticed me coming close to him, turned his back while he entered the car adjusting himself in his seat and started the engine.

I even entered the car and occupied the seat next to him, while I placed my bag on my lap and buckled my seat belt while holding the blue diary. I suppose the whole ride would be spending in silence. During short time intervals we both used to look at each other and would show fake smile as if assuring for the moment that everything is fine. While he was driving I noticed some rough marks on his knuckles as if he fought with someone.

But all could judge was Ayan's eye were full with redness, his eyes depict some pain. All I could console myself is things don't always go your way and that was something I had to remind myself often.

I gathered all my courage and panted softly, "Ayan I need to ask something to you."

As soon as I said those words which were quite audible to him, Ayan turned on the radio placed in the car at a high volume. As if he wanted to neglect my voice. This gesture definitely made me angry but all could do was drop a tear from my eye.

This time even I did not feel to talk to him, so I adjusted myself in my seat so that my elbow was rested against the window side and I titled my head enough so as to make Ayan notice that now even I was avoiding him.

It was early morning, while titling my head enough so that I could have a great view of the scenery outside. I could visualize that the twilight melted away, spreading the sunrise all over pinkish glow, clouds tinted, and colors spread across the sky, orange and red painted all across the sky.

The powerful sunrays flooded over the landscape lighting every blade of grass, making shine each and every leaf. Every new bud blossomed turning in a bright flower. There some freshness in the air. I felt the day was different and god has carved this day for me exclusively.

The silence between us was just driving me insane. I constantly glanced at my wrist, the hours were running faster. I had to talk to Ayan, dam it. And the more I wanted to, the more he was ignoring me. It was killing me and my patience.

After thinking about it for a while, I realized I didn't blame him for not talking to me. I should understand how he must have been feeling. He must be even confused about everything. He must not be finding the right words to talk or must be having an inside battle with himself. He must be thinking what I must be feeling about him.

"Shhh… more confusion started running in my mind. Because of frustration I started playing with my phone. So many thoughts were playing games in my mind that slowly I started shivering because of nervousness.

Felt as if all of a sudden I am stupid in this world. My fate is making fun of me. Everything happened in a fraction of second between us. I alone was not responsible for last night. If it was a mistake then we both were responsible not alone me. I alone should not only suffer the ignorance. I have a right to talk to him and clear certain things between us.

My anger started boiling off. I was aware Ayan would not pay attention on my words. So I had to do something so that he talks to me. There were massive thoughts that were floating in my head. All I wanted to speak to him and spill the beans as soon as possible which were disturbing Ayan so much.

Turning my head towards him, squinted my eyes to figure out what's wrong with him. All I could sense was a certain level of irritation making his face red, grumping with his fingers on the steering of the car. I didn't realize that was I madder at the situation or he is mad more than me.

Even though I really didn't feel of disturbing the comfort zone of Ayan, but now it was necessary to talk to him and understand his creepiness. I waited for another five minutes before actually regaining my energy and slowly stretching my arm towards him while touching his shoulder and making him sense that even I do exist in the car.

Enough of his acting, I was very well aware even he wanted to talk to me. This avoidance was just an uneasiness behavior which I was tolerating since morning. At times people act weird or in precise word they act nonsense, and so was Ayan since morning.

As soon as I placed my hand on his shoulder to divert his sense towards me, his body became stiff and eyes widened up bright with fear, he soon collected his senses and applied a tremendous pressure on the gear while increasing the speed of the car. The speed of the car was double its speed. Due to high speed the air was hitting are faces. As a result of excessive air the blue diary which was laying down my lap opened up and pages started turning up making a lot of noise of the pages thrashing to each other.

This attitude made me drive crazy. Now it was the last limit. My anger reached at its last stage, now I was very well aware I need to take my stand all alone. Demanding an explanation was my right.

That very moment I quickly placed my hand at the gear and applied a reverse force on it so that Ayan quickly looses its balance on the speed of the car and so was the case. In no time Ayan lost the control and applying all his energy he started moving the steering round and round, more round and round while the car even started revolving round on its own axis, making our head and body shake along the car turning on its axis.

He tried harder to gain control on the car again but he could not succeed and the car skid off the road and was about to hit the tree trunk which was nearby, before it could hit the tree truck within fractions of seconds Ayan was able to control the speed of the car and applied immense pressure on the breaks and stopped it before it could hit the trunk.

As the car came on a standstill, my gesture was terrifying. My eyes popped out due to dread, my hair were all messy and all over my face and my mouth was a bit open due to shock, while every heartbeats struggling with each other to beat faster and breathes were countless. Saw death so close my eyes pulling me in the tree trunk.

As soon as I gained my senses the first thing that my nerves of the brain ordered was Ayan. I quickly waved a look towards Ayan, and before I could speak Ayan interrupted, "Are you alright, Tasha." That very moment Ayan had tears in his eyes, sweat all over his face and I am sure heartbeats increased manifold times than mine.

By staring all over me, he made his judgment that I'm all fine and mumbled, "Thank God, you are fine, felt as if for a second God would have taken my life and saved you" while the tears started rolling down his cheeks with his hands praying to God for sending gratitude to him.

Rolling my eyes at his cheesiness but, truthfulness, a smile blossomed on my face. At Ayan's caring and gentle nature I lifted my tongue slightly up while widening my eyes in amusement with his kindness. "What?" I asked curiously as to why he reacted the way he did.

"What, what… you are saying. I am concerned about you; it's natural to get tensed in such a situation." While this much of saying he unblocked his seat belt and opened the door of the car and stepped out of it.

Letting loose a small laugh, I looked at him with an ironic smile. Within the same couple of seconds even I unblocked my seat belt and stepped out of the car. Moving towards him with a hope for getting the answer, which I was eager to hear. In the meantime he was busy searching something in the bags which were kept at the backside seat of the car.

His impatiently searching made me force to ask him, "What are searching? Can I help you?"

But as expected a rude answer with a rude tone was thrown on me, "No thanks, I'll help my self."

Struggling hard to find something in the bag, and unzipping almost all the three bags kept behind. My curiosity pushed me to tell him, "wait I'll help you to find but before that please let me know what you need."

"Water to quench my thirst" he answered in a low tone.

I dragged the bag from his hands towards me and pushed him a bit aside from the car so that I could remove the bottle comfortably.

While moving a bit aside from me, Ayan was standing quietly, while I happen to glanced at him from the corner of my eyes with simultaneously keeping the search engine on for the bottle. All I observed was that, Ayan was quiet and tensed also. A fierce battle was going in his so called brains. He was hiding something in his fake expression. His eyes were frequently rolling down in disbelief and making him conscious about something. Some pain, some emotion, some truth was hidden beneath his eyes.

That something feeling was eating everything thing in him. In the mean time my search engine stopped and the bottle was in my hand and I offered to him. While taking the bottle in his hand he said, "Thanks" and moved away from the car to the other side of the road.

Opened the lid of the bottle and quenched his thirst, while pouring certain quantity of water in his palm and splashing them on his face to get fresh. I was standing at the

Ruchi Bhandari

opposite side of the road near the car, engaged in watching his actions. It made me feel as we are two different poles standing opposite to each other, willing to get attracted but some power is stopping us.

The more I looked at him the more my love for him would amplify. A relationship can only sustain if there is trust in one another's eyes. Every relationship begins with trust and dwells in a constant strive to fulfill it. I don't know why that trust was lacking between us. Something was missing somewhere.

Missing something... supposing tears in my eyes. This thought was as irritating as a flicking tube light. It's very ironical the person who gives you a lot of happiness is the only person who can give you a lot tears.

Ayan standing at the other side of the road, for couple of seconds peered at me. His glaze met my gaze. A hope of ray pooped out in my heart, "might be this time he will answer my all queries" I consoled myself.

I was standing leaning to the car. Playing with my fingers, my phone rang and vibrated which was laying down on the blue diary in the car. Hearing the phone tone I turned myself and peered from the window of the car to my phone. There was an incoming call from Jiya.

I answered the call, "Hello".

Jiya replied, "Hello, how are you? I received miscall form your number."

"Umm...yes I called to inform you that I'll be reaching home today evening." I stated in a low tone.

"Is everything fine Tasha, you are sounding low." She added.

I tried to plaster a fake smile on my face with real tears in my eyes controlling them to flow, while gulped my saliva responded, "Yes everything alright, just a bit tired."

Before she would respond further, I continued saying, "Will talk to you later, battery is about to die." And hanged up the call.

Was about to place my phone in the car back to its original place, suddenly my eyes struck to the blue diary. The blue diary contained all sort of emotional poems which had the influence or I must say command to suit on any situation.

Whosoever the writer may be, I must say must have suffered from tremendous pain in his life, which made the person to expose, such beautiful words in the form of rhymes. The words where craved as such, which I willing read in a loud voice. So that it was audible to Ayan, who was behaving absurd and rude form morning.

KHAMOSHI

Kyu khamosh ho tum humse…Jane kya raaz chupa rahe ho…
Khudko sazza sekar…mujhe bhi tadpa rahe ho…
Pyar tho hua hai tumse…Ye tho tum bhi jaan gaye ho…
Fir najre churakar kyu…Jhakam bada rahe ho…

While I was reading those lines I looked up for a quick look at Ayan, just to make sure my voice is audible to him.

While I was reading these lines, Ayan turned towards me and was quietly listening to rhymes. Further I could read the next stanza Ayan interrupted, with a voice carrying a depth of sorrow in his heart.

Tumhare sathne mujhe mere…sare gam bhula diye…
Fir iss tarah wapas kyu …mujhe gam diye ja rahe ho…
Tumhare tezz dhadkan ki …awaz mai bhi mehsoos kar raha hu…

Stunned by the words, as the same words appeared on the page. Before I could raise my gaze from the book to Ayan, he further continued in his depressed voice. All I could visualize was lots of anger, loneliness and some guilt on his face. He wanted to cry out loud but his inner self was not allowing him to do. Some situation made him so stiff that his tears even did not will to flow. Voice had some crackling sounds as if the person was internally crying.

He further continued,

Kya ye…
Kya ye mere liye hai bas…yahi soch raha hu…
Baat karo mujhse mat satao…itna ke mai gamo me doob jau…
Kahi aisa na ho… ke wapas laut ke bhi naa aa pau…

"Am I troubling you? Why are not answering my question? Since morning I'm being running behind you just to know what's going in your useless brains", I replied in an irritating gesture.

Ayan was standing clueless in this discussion. Folding his both hands at his chest he was just peering at me with no swords of words. It felt as if he was capturing me in his eyes for the rest of his life.

I felt as if some unforeseen will happen. My inner soul was speaking, "Tasha stop this time. Heart was beating fast. The train was running, my soul was weeping and sayings go catch hold. The more I hold the sand the more the sand was slipping form my hand." Various thoughts occupied space in my mind.

What to do or what not to do? With such confusion basically I just lifted my foot ahead and started walking towards Ayan. My eyes were constantly fixed at Ayan. Except him I could not feel anything, could not hear anything, and could not see anything. All my senses were totally numb. I took larger steps to reach fast towards him.

Horn! Horn! Horn!

Horn! Horn! Horn!

Ayan's words

I tried to clean my cheeks from the waterworks that were falling from my eyes. The drive to the hospital had felt like the longest drive of my life. My fingers did not have life in them. Due to fear and blood all over me and my hands I could not apply pressure on the steering of the car. But I had to drive fast very fast.

Everything will be okay. Everything will be okay was the only mantra I repeated to myself. I peered at the backseat where Tasha was laying unconscious in blood. There were lots of bruises on her body. Her half side of body was totally damaged and number of cuts and scratches all over. She looked lifeless.

Oh God please....

Oh God please....

Oh God please....

Save her I promise I'll tell her the truth. Please!!!! Don't cruse her for my sin.

Calm down Ayan…She will be fine soon…

I consoled myself abruptly rubbing my hands on my head while increasing the speed of the car from 80 to 100 to 120 to 140.

Horn!!! Side!!! Move!!! Horn!!! Horn!!! Horn!!!

Just when you want to reach somewhere very soon the biggest obstacle one could ever face is the green light turning red and there you have stop. The traffic signal never follow your instructions and nor do I followed its instruction this time. I just drove and drove really fast.

Halt to the hospital – the stretcher carries Tasha in the operation theatre – doctors rushing – red light on – and Tasha fighting for her life.

She has to be okay. She has to be okay. She will be okay. I kept on repeating this over and over. The more I tried to convince myself the more level of pain in my heart started to grow.

I can't lose her…I can't lose her…

Removing my phone from my back pocket; dialed the number of Jiya to inform her about the accident. I sniffed before talking to Jiya, "Tasha – accident – hospital" all I could say to her. She could barely speak, "Wh –aa -t" started to cry.

"M coming" as she hang up the call. I slide the phone and placed it back in my pocket again. Moving to and fro outside the operation theatre; praying continuously. I felt my heart is sinking. She can't leave her family. She can't leave the restaurant business. She can't leave me. She can't leave me. I don't want that.

Jiya and Aunty arrived. Both of their noses turned red due to continuous tears flowing down. Aunty could barely speak. While Jiya was totally numb standing near the door of the operation theatre; waiting for the doctors to come out.

I hugged aunty and sat next to her. Jiya walked closed to me and asked "Did the doctors say anything about her?"

I shook my head and answered, "Doctors are examining her form last forty five minutes. All they can say is Trust God."

As minutes passed by and we waited, I informed Samir's dad about the whole scenario. His immediate answer was, "God please be kind to Tasha…I already lost my son now I don't want to lose my daughter." This line made me feel as if somebody has punched me hard. All I could say is "PRAY…Uncle." He offered to help but I politely refused as it was necessary for him to be at restaurant. At least one of us should be present in the restaurant.

Countless doctors had walked in and out. We all waiting eagerly to answer our query but none of them were ready to talk, they just rushed in and out. All we could do is to wait and wait. After an hour or so one of the doctors approaches us. Finally will hear something from him about Tasha (whether good or bad but something for sure).

"Mr. Ayan" he painted.

"Umm…yes doctor? I sniffled while my eyes started to fill with tears.

"She has several bruised ribs, a number of cuts on her whole body and her left arm is been totally fractured due to impact of the vehicle. Nevertheless, her brain activities are stable and normal so we expect her to recover soon. Must say she was lucky, that her brain did not get damage like the rest of her body. She has been shifted from the theatre to the other ward for rest. You people may visit her for few minutes but please make sure you don't disturb the patient. Rest is all she needs" the doctor explained with a forceful smile.

"Huh!!! A sign of relief was felt by all of us. The huge weight of terror on our heart and mind was replaced with relief. We all thanked the doctor and proceeded towards Tasha's room.

I let Jiya and aunt go first. I sat on a bench outside the room having guilt of all my sin. Every incident or you may say my sin was clearly standing in front of me. The more I thought the guiltier I was feeling. If I had told her sooner, this wouldn't have happened ever. I only allowed things to go this far before I decided to tell her. I felt incredibly disgusting about myself. I silently cried before entering her room.

I would have never forgiven myself if she had died. At this moment of time I have to confess her the truth. She has to know the reason of my coming her. The secret which was deep in the dark has now to come in the light.

Waiting outside desperately for Jiya and aunt to come out; they have the very first right to see her. Till time I gathered all the courage to tell her truth. I don't care whether she will forgive me or not. Might be she will never see me again or might be she will hurt herself but for now it's important for her to know the truth.

"Oh!!! Lord please help me" I prayed on and on.

"I'll drop mom and return back till time you please be here and take care of Tasha" Jiya spoke while exiting the room along with aunt.

"It's okay. Ill just go in and see her. I'll be here the whole night with Tasha; you just take care of aunty at this moment." I replied hugging aunty.

I lightly opened the door of the room, closing it quietly. She was unconscious. Several cables and wires were attached to her body, keeping track of her heart beats, the left side was totally damaged. I walked to the edge of her bedside and pulled a chair, sitting next to her and reached to her hand to hold it. Dull face with several stitch on her body. The reassuring beeping of the heart monitor was the only evidence of her being still alive.

As I held her hand, I squeezed and rubbed her hand. I brought her hand to my lips and kissed it gently as a tear started to fall and I murmured, "I'm so sorry. For being stupid since morning – sorry for no telling you the truth – sorry for the accident – sorry for all the pain which I gave you – sorry for every sin – sorry for everything." I swallowed the guzzle forming in my throat as I held back the shed tears and continued talking "but please come back. I need you. I love you too."

The Truth

(Part – II)

*T*asha's unconsciousness

Sometimes I could feel the pain striking in my head. Rest of the times, I would feel numbness all over me. My periods of consciousness were short. I kept coming in and out of unconsciousness. During my conscious periods I could hear barely audible words and whispers echoed in the room. Some voices and touches I could recognize well others were difficult to understand. I could hear the constant beeping of the machine and feel number of cables and wires attached to my skin.

One of the conscious moments, I felt someone hold my hand; it was Ayan for sure. I can recognize his touch. A moister droplet falls on my skin; tear. I felt Ayan's lip kissed my hand. His voice was also audible, the words which he spurted out, "I need you. I love you…" was all I wanted him to say. It's a relief to know that my feelings aren't one sided. If I was not tied with these cables and wires I would have jumped on bed and danced for his sweet confession and hugged him tightly.

I wanted to comfort him, but was unable to open my eyes. My body has become weak and I guess it will take time to recover. Still I gathered all my courage to open my eyelids. I gazed at him and uttered, "I LOVE YOU TOO." He smiles at my reaction while sobbing his throat.

"I need to confession something. After hearing that you won't love me anymore" he speaks.

"W-what? Nothing can change my love for you" I defended.

He grins at my reaction. "I have a bit of explaining to do. It's just not u & me. But it's U Me and Fate."

"Please. Explain." I say desperately seeking my answer.

He grips my palm tightly in his before beginning, sending my heart into overdrive again. It felt as if he thought after hearing his confession I will never hold him. But for me it felt as if my heart will jump out and will land on my bed; and it will all be his fault.

"I'm not good at this whole admitting feelings and all so you'll have to forgive me if it doesn't come out right" he response.

Who bothers; just shoot fast as this confession, suspense is killing me within. I did not speak those words but it was all what I was thinking. Instead I just decided to nod and wait for him to speak.

"Six years back. The party night; where Samir was invited. As it was a common friends blast even I was present for the party." He explains every minute detail as if it was necessary at all.

Wait, did he say he was also present at the party? How did it never strike me that Ayan might even be invited for the same party where Samir was? Might be I would have got some information of the accident night early only.

"Anyways, you remember Roma? The one, we met at Mr. David's business party. She studied with us during our hotel management course. The fact that she was not only pretty, beautiful, gorgeous etc but also someone different from the other girls. She drove us crazy completely. Both I and Samir had a bet you could win over her heart first. After a couple of hanging around and date she ended up selecting me."

"A girl; whom both Samir and Ayan liked." I stated a bit loudly. I really need to stop screaming on that. He looks at me with regret while nodding answered, "Yeah I did love her & Samir had lust for her. For me she was never a competition to win over but actually a girl with whom I could spend the rest of my life forever and ever."

"So suddenly what went wrong?" I reacted while adjusting myself to sit up erect. I tried to remove my hand from his hand but he squeezes them and helped me to sit though still continuing to hold my hand.

"Samir went wrong." He said viciously.

Samir doing something wrong; I don't agree. I uttered it to myself.

"We had been together for almost six month; our relationship was at its peak. But...once a friend threw a party at his place; I brought her too along. Roma and I had been both drinking quite heavily. It was not the first time we both were drinking but that day it was different. I started feeling very weird. I never felt that way before from drinking; but could not figure out what was wrong in the drinks. I just don't remember anything else about that night and the next thing I knew the next morning was I ended up on a bed with my other classmate."

An o-o-o formed on my face; while letting out a gasp I asked, "Did you sleep with her?"

I could not understand anything but hearing this incident was making me angering and confused.

"What? No. I can never do wrong with any girl. Except Roma I never ever saw any girl that way." He quickly replied in disgust.

"Then what happened?" I replied with a smirk might be not believing on his story.

"Roma happened to be there at the right place in the right time in the wrong situation to see all this. It was someone who had mixed something in my drinks and I knew because I had been drunk enough times to know that it wasn't only alcohol at all. He shrugs while recollecting the moment. I tried to explain – I begged – I wept a number of times but she did not respond except saying one deadly sentence "it's all over" and she left.

After that she avoided my calls my messages for days and the last news I heard was Samir and Roma dating each other. After that news I did not bother to disturb them at all. After all it was her decision to apart and I can't force her to stay. If she stays then she was always mine; and if she leaves then she was never mine.

I wanted to give him comfort and tell him how sorry I was feeling but all I could do is I squeezed his palm to offer my concern. I was getting the answer of my question; that is it – this was the main reason why Samir never bother to tell me about Ayan.

My head was trying to process this access information which I'd just received. In the meantime the most important questions arose in my mind was "Than why did you come here back to help Samir's dad? What was the purpose behind his help to us? Was he taking revenge from us? My curiosity started increasing rapidly. So I guess finally I get my answer.

"I arrived at the party that night. During conversation with out classmate Samir spurted out the truth in front of everyone that he only mixed drugs in my drink." His face turned red while reciting the whole incident.

"Is it?" I ask in shock.

He nods, "Yeah! After the party got over I met Samir near the highway. It was approximately 1.00 am. My whole intention was to throw a hard punch on Samir's face for the blunder he created in my life.

Samir on the other hand, stood there casually with an amused playful smile.

Well...What harm did I do to you? Why the hell did you mess up my life? I asked in a calm voice to Samir.

"No harm you did. But the girl wasn't right for anyone of us." Samir sneered.

"She was right; you turned her bad." I groaned.

Samir's eyes glistened with a crooked smile, "She needed to be used… so man… I just did it."

With those words, I just aimed my fist directly to Samir's face.

Samir caught hold my fist in his grip with a grin on his face.

The very next moment I punched hard on his stomach. Samir lost the grip and was holding his ached stomach.

Before he could get stable I snapped his head so fast making sure a crack would appear in his head. His cheeks turn red with fury; his just managed to push hard his elbow straight in my neck.

We were now exactly at the middle of the road.

By hearing this much my hand were shaking. Although Samir was a bad boy ever I heard from some common friends but he would turn so violent for a bet made me shocked. After me coming in his life I never heard of him getting into any sort of fights.

Lost in my own thought; Ayan squeezed my hand while rubbing the upper surface of my hand with his eyes filled with water he started the rest of the story.

His leg aimed at my lungs making my balance lose and fall on the road. "Why the hell; who are fighting for a girl who isn't even worth for anything?"

I got up in seconds and quickly threw a punch at Samir's face and stated in agony, "God Dam it…I loved that girl and I just lost her because of you." He screamed in agony because of the punch.

I could not judge right and wrong; Samir or Ayan. Both occupied a special place in my heart. Samir being my first love; while Ayan made me fall in love with him; that time when I lost all the hopes in my life. On the verge of tears, I gathered my strength and met his wet eyes and said, "Than what happened next."

Ayan continued, "Before Samir could get steady I did a roundhouse kick to his stomach; with that kick he was pushed at the centre of the road while holding his both hands on his stomach he screamed in pain. Seeing him in pain I had a smile lingering on my face.

"Get up, you pervert!" I winked.

He balanced to stand up; at that very moment his phone rang. He action his hand saying me stop the fight. Till the time he attended the call a truck arrived and blow him off. "S-s-samir" I shouted.

A gasp escaped my lips, "Ah, shit." I winced after hearing. A shiver ran down my spine, I knew he was dead but nevertheless; I didn't want him to die this way.

"Calm down!" Ayan muttered while rubbing my hand in the same pattern he did before.

I frowned at him, while removing my hand forcefully from his hand, "Calm down, are you crazy. You knew what went wrong with Samir during the accident; since days you are staying with us but you never ever utter anything about the accident."

He froze in shock.

"I'm mad; I thought you even feel the way I feel for you. But I was stupid... to know that you are sitting with me because of your guilt." I continued, "this is what you say......U ME & FATE."

It's a fact I responded while crying, "When the cause of all causes becomes known, then everything knowable becomes know, & nothing remains unknown." Today suddenly all my questions which were deep buried in my heart gets their respective answers. Can't judge you – you came as an angel – but you will leave as a demon. Can't make out should I love you or shall I hate you.

"Listen to me" he pleaded while sobbing.

"No… don't you dare! Even utter a word" I responded aggressively while pulling all the cables and wires attached to me. All you're caring, your love, your help, and your affection was bogus. If all of that was fake then I must say you are a master at deceiving people.

"God…Damm…Don't remove those from your body. I know I did wrong but please don't harm your self. You have just been operated." He requested while holding my hands from doing so.

"Leave me" I commented in disgust. Struggling to escape form his tight grip it is that time he holds me tight from my waist and brings me close to him. Before I know what was happening Ayan's lips crash down on mine consuming my every thought and I immediately lose up my defense. His soft lips started rubbing my lips with so much love, passion, affection and many more that I felt like I can forgive every crime.

When he pulls away; the tears rolling down from my cheeks till my neck quickly. My mind is still focused on the confession while the heart says to forgive.

Mind – Anger v/s Heart – Love

I moved back form him, while I closed my eyes shut and crouched down against the bed. Covering my face with my hands while bring my legs closed to my chest. And just hating myself for not knowing what to do or what not to do?

I just knew it was all my fate. It is again the fate that binds and breaks.

"God please, please help me…help me…help me" I grunt in pain.

Ayan came close to me; placing his warm hands gently on my hands while trying to uncover my face. I lifted my gaze up to meet his gaze, "Ayan" my voice was barely audible to him, and I just buried my face into his chest and hugged him tightly.

While sobbing he replied, "It was just an accident Tasha!!! Definitely I was angry on him but I never thought to kill him. Please trust me. If you'll say to leave – I'll leave. But please don't hurt your self."

"I never wanted to let you know this truth, but the first time I saw you in the church – my guilt arrived at its edge. I found you helpless towards your life.

You were weeping in agony.

That day I decided, to help you." He commented with tears in his eyes.

Sometimes, you begin to think about something after its finish.

He began to leave.

STOP….

Don't go.

I don't want to be alone again.

I cried out loud.

He rushed towards me and embraced me in his arms.

☺☺☺☺☺☺☺☺☺☺